Being Youngest

DISCARD

Being Youngest

JIM HEYNEN

HarperTrophy®
A Division of HarperCollinsPublishers

HarperTrophy® is a registered trademark of HarperCollins Publishers Inc.

Being Youngest
Copyright © 1997 by Jim Heynen

ISBN: 0-380-73204-1
Library of Congress Catalog Card Number: 97-9366
First HarperTrophy edition, 2000

Visit us on the World Wide Web!
www.harperchildrens.com

10 9 8 7 6 5 4 3 2 1

For Sally Williams

———

In memory of John Engman, poet and friend, 1949–1996

Special thanks to Bill and Nancy Booth for their support and kind provi-sions at Cry of the Loon Lodge on Kabekona Lake, where, in the dead of winter, much of this book was written; and to Diane Friend and the crew at Caffè Con Amore, where, in all kinds of weather, much of this book was revised. Also, my thanks to Steve Polansky, Ruth Bly, and Steve Sanfield who read early versions and gave many useful suggestions; and to my niece Laurie Buyert, sister Carolyn Van Beek, and sister-in-law Joyce Heynen, who provided me with a few crucial reminders on animal husbandry, Iowa cooking, and rural childhood.

Table of Contents

Being Youngest

ONE

A Taste of the Worst

HENRY LIVED ON A FARM with his father, two older brothers, and his grandmother. Being the youngest person in this arrangement meant that you always got the short end of the stick. The dirty end. It wasn't just that he had to wear hand-me-down clothes, or that his older brothers pushed him around as if he were some kind of unbreakable toy, or that he was the only kid in the county whose mother had died when he was four. Maybe a boy could handle all of that if it weren't for Granny. Granny tipped the scales in more ways than one. Not only was she the meanest and laziest old lady in the world, but she was a real fatso. A waddler, if you want to put it nice. She ate so much and she did so little that she was like a big loaf of bread dough that stands out too long and keeps rising and pretty soon it's bulging up over the edge of the mixing bowl. Everything Granny sat in was like a mixing bowl, what with her bulging up over the edge of whatever she decided to stuff herself into.

People said Henry was the quiet one in the family, and usually he was—unless something so terrible was done to him that he had no choice but to speak up. Henry had figured out that if you are youngest and if you have any wits about you at all, you can stay out of a lot of trouble by doing more thinking than talking. The way he saw it, the only safe place to get things out in the open was inside your own head with your mouth closed, just thinking. If you kept your mouth shut, you could ask any question you wanted to. Why, for instance, didn't his father find some sort of house-keeper who was about the same age his mother had been? Or why didn't his father send him off to live with his aunt? Either of those choices would have been better than Granny. But, oh no, to make matters as bad as they could be on this earth, his father had decided that Granny would live in the house, in the basement by night and upstairs by day, until the boys grew up.

Until the boys grew up. Some growing anybody could do with the likes of Granny around. When she did manage to get up and walk, she looked like she was carrying two ten-gallon water balloons on her backside. And she wasn't much better from the front. Her cheeks were so big and heavy they looked like a couple of wrinkled pancakes that could fall off her face if she shook her head fast. But she was strong when she wanted to be, and if she was really angry her thick arms and big hands could swing out quick as a cow's tail and swat you a good one. At least Henry could outrun her, if it ever came to that.

It hadn't come to that yet but the summer was just getting started. Henry had looked around inside his head for a good summer plan, and he had come up with one—he'd stay outside all day, stay clear of ole Granny all the time except when it was time to eat. But today not even that plan was working out. He'd gone outside to play all right, but then he'd gotten into this little game with his older brothers, throwing corncobs at one another. It was a good enough game with no sides, just everybody for himself. A hit on the leg and you have to cripple, a hit on the arm and you can't use that arm, a hit in the back and you have to crawl, a hit in the head and you're dead—out of the game.

Things hadn't gone well. As usual his older brothers picked on him. They wanted Henry to get hurt so he'd quit playing and leave them alone. That's what the corncob game was really all about. So Henry had gotten hurt, and now he was moping along across the stinking farmyard, kicking dirt. His left elbow oozed blood where a corncob had clipped him, and his knees hurt because his brothers pushed him down when he wouldn't stay dead like they said he was supposed to.

Times like this he really had no choice but to go to the house and take his chances with Granny, what with his dad out in the back of the field cultivating corn.

He swung open the screen door and yelled, "What's to eat?"

Just as loud Granny yelled back, "Don't let the flies in!"

He pulled the screen door shut quickly.

"And don't slam the door!"

That's the way Granny was. She'd get you coming or going. Henry walked into the kitchen, and there she was, plopped down and filling up his dad's swivel chair by the kitchen window.

"I'm hungry," he said, keeping his range in case she was in one of her cranky morning moods.

"Milk in the refrigerator," she said. She looked him over. "And what have you done to yourself this time?"

As if she cared.

Henry knew better than to tell anybody what really happened to him. Tattling is one of the bad things littlest kids are supposed to do, but you learn not to tattle on the big kids because if you do the big kids beat you up. Either that or the big kids tattle back on you for tattling and you end up catching it from both sides at once.

"Nothin," he said.

"You better put something on that arm," Granny said, and grunted her way out of the chair.

"Where are your brothers?"

"What brothers?" he said. Then he watched her. This was the sort of thing that could get him in trouble. But she wasn't coming at him. She was putting her hands on her hips and pushing down, as if maybe this was going to keep her top part from falling off.

He poured himself a glass of milk.

"Don't go spilling," said Granny.

Henry swirled the milk around in the glass, letting it get really close to the top without spilling. Granny tried to scare him with her semi-with-the-headlights-turned-on look, but it didn't work. And Henry didn't spill, at least not enough for anybody to have a fit about.

"Got a cookie?" he said.

"No cookies," said Granny, but he could smell that something was brewing in the oven. He knew better than to ask what. If Granny did anything special, she always wanted it to be a surprise. If anybody knew she was baking something, it spoiled her fun, Henry guessed. This was just one of the weird things about Granny.

Henry downed his milk and walked into the front room to the old piano and plunked out the song he had been working on, "Indian Dance." It used both hands. *Thum thum thum thum* went the Indian drums with his left hand, and *pink pink pink pink* went the Indians dancing with his right hand.

The sweet smells from the oven were getting stronger. He played the song again, a little louder.

When he finished, he sniffed toward the kitchen. It was something chocolate. He remembered that smell from when he was just a very little boy and his mother would cook something with chocolate in it. But she never hid it. She let him look at what she was cooking so long as he didn't touch the hot stove. Not Granny.

Once more for "Indian Dance," he decided, and then

Granny should be ready to surprise him with whatever she had going in the oven.

"Enough!" yelled Granny as he pounded away one more time on "Indian Dance." "Enough! Outside! Now!"

Henry shuffled toward the porch door but kept an eye on the oven.

"You see it and you don't get any," she said.

"I don't see nothin," he said, and kept going.

And he hadn't seen anything. But he had smelled it. More than chocolate, it was fudge! Now all he had to do was make sure he didn't spoil Granny's fun. Surprising people was the only thing that could put Granny in a decent mood.

Outside, there was really nothing to do but look for his brothers. He could try to find something to do by himself, but he knew they'd be having the most fun, and that wasn't fair. He set out to find them.

There they were in the grove—big Jake and middle-sized Josh—having a good time on the play farm. They were crawling around on their hands and knees, pushing tractors and wagons through fields that they had marked off with pretend fence wire made out of baling twine and pretend fence posts made out of Popsicle sticks. Their blue jeans had been clean this morning. Now Henry could see the knees were getting caked with dirt from the good time they were having crawling around. Getting clean clothes dirty like that was the sort of thing that would get him in trouble with Granny, but she probably wouldn't bother his brothers about it. They were like her pets, and she'd let them get away with anything. Henry wondered sometimes if maybe Granny was just a little bit afraid of them. Why else would she let them get away with things she'd never put up with from Henry? Granny would just as soon swat him as look at him. And she could get away with it. Henry knew how to take his licks, whether he deserved them or not. He took them because if he didn't, everybody would make him feel like an even bigger baby than he already was.

"Get outta here," said big Jake in his nasty voice.

"I can play here too," said Henry. "Granny says."

"Sure, 'Granny says,'" said middle-sized Josh. "Granny says, 'Go play with your head in the toilet.'"

"Go play on the stupid piano," Jake said, and held out his dirty hands like somebody who was about to come down on piano keys. "Go play 'Little Boy Blue.'"

"Go blow your horn somewhere else," said Josh.

Henry stood against a box elder tree watching his brothers play. Big brother Jake was really getting too old for this sort of thing. He was almost a foot taller than Henry and four inches taller than Josh. The only thing the three of them shared was their mousy brown hair and their big eyebrows and long eyelashes—just like their father's. Old big-shot Jake was starting to get some pale hairs above his lip. Pretty soon he should start looking at girls instead of toy tractors on a play farm. Let him grow up and get out of the way—the sooner the better, as far as Henry was concerned. If Jake was out of the way, Henry could fill in the space he'd leave and be down on his knees right now having fun on the play farm.

Henry stood watching. His brothers had real toy tractors and wagons—and farm buildings made out of shingles. They had taken some mown grass from the lawn and scattered it over the ground inside the toy fences. Now they were going around with kitchen forks, scooping the grass off the ground and loading it into the wagon. They were haying, that's what they were doing. They were going to haul this hay in the wagon to the little wooden barn. They were having more fun than anyone in the whole world.

"I'm gonna tell Granny you took forks from the kitchen," said Henry.

"Do and we'll stick you with the blame," said old blubber-face Jake.

"Do and we'll stick your head in a cowpie," said Josh. The dust in the corners of his mouth got wet when he talked like that and turned to mud. Mud-face Josh.

Henry left them there on their stupid old farm. For being so cruel, his brothers weren't going to find out that Granny was fixing a surprise. He strolled toward the house. "Dumb balls," he muttered, and gave the stuffy air a couple of good punches. "Stupid egghead dumb balls."

Then he thought of the fudge. Maybe he'd get a look through the kitchen window and see how it was doing. The old yellow dog Buster saw him and came wagging toward him. Good old Buster, you could always count on him to be in a good mood.

"Yeah, Bus. Bussy Bussy Bussy," he said, and gave the big dog's ears a good rubbing. Buster ran ahead a little ways and then back, ahead a little ways and then back.

Granny was ready when Henry got to the kitchen. There on the table a whole mound of fudge was stacked on a sheet of wax paper.

"Wow! Fudge!"

"Surprised?" said Granny.

"Never so surprised in my whole life!"

Granny smiled, she actually smiled.

"Two for everybody," she said. "Where are your brothers?"

"On the play farm," he said.

"Can you make it to the grove with all of these pieces?"

"Just watch," he said.

Henry took the fudge and headed toward the grove, where the older boys were having their good time. He took a shortcut through the alleyway of the corncrib. When Jake and Josh see this pile of fudge, they'll let me play with them for sure, he thought.

He stopped in the corncrib alley to see which piece was biggest. He could make sure he got the biggest piece himself without ruining the surprise for his brothers. But Granny had made every piece exactly the same size. He rearranged the fudge on the wax paper, but he couldn't tell one piece from the next. Granny had been that careful to make sure nobody was going to be fighting over who got the biggest piece.

Then Henry got the idea that he'd take just a nibble

off the corner of the top piece. He started out slowly the way he always started out slowly with the first piece of candy on Christmas, letting it rest on his tongue and moving it around in his mouth to get all the taste. This fudge was Granny at her best. He laid the piece back and got ready to carry the stack to his brothers.

Then Henry saw a problem. This wasn't the first time in his life that he'd noticed how bad times always seem to come right when you think you're in the middle of the good times. But there it was, a problem just when things were looking good, or at least tasting good. Now that bit-off piece of fudge stuck out like an untied shoestring. Henry decided he'd solve this problem by taking a little bite off each one to make them look alike, but when he did this, things just got worse. Fingerprints. Uneven shapes. Teeth marks. No doubt about it, the harder he worked to straighten things out, the worse they got. He pressed and squeezed, but the fudge was like model clay in school when you can never get it back exactly the way you had it. It was worse than model clay. It was like trying to rub out the finger mark you just made on the frosting of somebody else's birthday cake.

It would have been one thing if Henry was doing something terribly wrong, but he wasn't. All he was doing was trying to make the pieces come out even. All he was doing was trying to keep his brothers from getting mad about a teensy-weensy little nibble he took off that first piece.

When Henry looked down at what was left on the

wax paper, the pieces of fudge looked like dog turds. This is what he got for trying so hard to make all the pieces come out even so that nobody would fight. He did the only thing he could think of—he put his hands on the fudge and prayed, "Oh God, please make them all even." When he opened his eyes, he saw that God wasn't going to have anything to do with the pickle he'd gotten himself into. To bring an end to this awful situation, he picked up the sad clumps of fudge, pressed them into a ball, and stuffed them in his mouth. He chewed and swallowed what was left with a loud *glnk*. Buster looked at him and raised an eyebrow that said, "Are you all right?"

He patted Buster on the head. Now that all the evidence was gone, he felt a little better. Once again, a bad time had come and gone. He wadded up the wax paper and stuffed it into a fresh rat hole that had just been dug in the alley. He licked his fingers clean. He stood there empty-handed. This isn't the way he had planned things to go, but he had done his best to make everything turn out all right, and he couldn't feel bad about that.

Now all he had to do was go to the play farm and bother his brothers long enough so that by the time they thought of going to the house, the cows would have to be milked and the idea of fudge anything would be the last thing on their minds. But it was too late to bother them. They were on their way to the house. "Come here, Bus," he said, and crouched down to watch them through the gaping slats of the corncrib.

His brothers went into the house and stayed there for what felt like a very long time. Then they came out carrying clean milk buckets. They were on their way to do chores.

Could this be happening? Could this *nothing* be happening? he wondered. Maybe finally in his life bad times weren't going to follow the good times. Maybe this is what getting older was all about, when finally you turn a corner, never again to be caught at a little mistake like eating all the fudge. Henry gave Buster a big hug. "Nothin's gonna happen," he said to the dog. "Nothin bad is gonna happen!"

And nothing bad did happen. At least not that night, before supper or after supper. Henry went to bed with his stomach a little fuller than usual, but he was feeling good about the world. The next morning started out on the right foot too. Granny yelled up the stairs, "Time to get up! Come on, Henry! I have a surprise!"

Two days in a row? It was almost nine o'clock, morning snack time, and everyone else had been up since early morning. This would be a great way for him to start the day. This was more of the good life that had started out yesterday when something bad might have happened and didn't. But when Henry stepped into the kitchen, he knew something wasn't quite right. His father was already back in the fields, but the three biggest problems of his life stood there with the kind of smiles he didn't want to see. Granny had a bag and pulled out a bunch of La Fama candy bars. If there was anything on earth as good as fudge, it was La Fama candy bars. She took the wrappers off with her pudgy fingers. Then, one at a time, she handed the two older boys each a La Fama candy bar. But Granny was one short. The older boys held theirs while Henry stood staring.

"There," said Granny in her fat pushy voice.

"Where's mine?" said Henry.

"You're not getting any, little boy," said Granny. "This is what happens to people who steal. Just stand there and watch."

They couldn't really be doing this to him. He had been tricked into hurrying downstairs for this? The older boys grinned, not just ordinary happy grins, but smirky grins that made their nostrils bigger. They broke their La Fama candy bars in half and held the two creamy halves toward Henry. They moved them back and forth under Henry's nose so that he turned his head from side to side. They were teasing him the same way they sometimes teased Buster by holding a dog biscuit under his nose and moving it back and forth without giving the dog a bite.

Tears burned their way over Henry's eyelids.

"You cry and you'll get a whupping to boot," said the tub of lard, and spit sputtered on her blubbery lips as she said that.

"It's not fair!" screamed Henry.

His mother would never have treated him like this. He was the littlest kid, what did they expect? His mother would have scolded him about eating all the fudge and then listened to his story. She would have understood how he tried to get all the pieces to come out even. Everybody knows how hard it is to straighten out one of those little mistakes. It was like trying to erase a color mark that goes outside the line by accident. It was exactly like that, and the harder you try to fix it, the more things get messed up. Things get away from you and you end up with a mess a good kid can't fix. His mother would have understood that.

"Yum yum," said slobbery-mouth Jake as he took his first bite from his La Fama candy bar.

"Buzzard!" shouted Henry. He didn't remember ever saying that word before. That word must have been waiting inside him like a mean dog locked in a doghouse, waiting for the right time to come out snarling. That time was now. He felt his mouth wanting to say it again, this time to that dimwit Josh.

"You be quiet!" shouted his grandmother, almost blowing her cheeks off. "Talk like that is just going to get you into bigger trouble. You learn your lesson good from this!"

"It's not fair! I couldn't get the pieces to come out even, so I had to eat them all!"

"Guess it's coming out even now," said fat-head Josh.

They were ganging up on him, sneers all the way around.

"You and your stupid surprise!" Henry yelled at Granny. "It's not fair!"

"Naht fay-er," teased fuzz-lip Jake.

"Dumb, stupid buzzards!" screamed Henry through his tears. "I'll kill all of you stupid, dumb buzzards! I hate you!" He swung his arms wildly at his brothers, but Granny made a quick waddle up behind him and grabbed him in her strong fat hands. He squirmed until he could pound against her blubbery stomach, while his gooey-faced brothers went on grinning and eating their La Fama candy bars. The worst had come, and the anger raging through Henry's mind didn't let him see a time when the worst would ever stop.

TWO

Gretchen Learns a Lesson

GRETCHEN LIVED WITH HER FATHER and mother and older sister on a farm a half mile from where Henry lived. Since Gretchen's family had just moved to Iowa from North Dakota right after school let out, the two had not yet met.

For Gretchen, the farm in Iowa was like an exciting new toy you get for Christmas and two weeks later it's no fun anymore. Iowa was supposed to be better than North Dakota, where her mother said they had almost gone broke. Maybe there was more money to be made in these cornfields than there was in the pastures and wheat fields of North Dakota, but Iowa wasn't everything it was cracked up to be—unless you liked the smell of hog manure at breakfast while you were trying to eat. The days were just as hot and muggy out here and the horseflies bit just as hard. And at night there were more mosquitoes than stars. Speaking of stars, where were the fireflies? North Dakota had a lot more of them.

So far, living in Iowa had been no picnic, and her family wasn't making life any easier—but then, they never had. There was her mother for starters. She was a tall, wiry woman with long fingers and a manner so jittery that she could make a biscuit nervous. It's not that Gretchen was the only person who noticed what a jitter-box her mother was. One time her father, who didn't say anything funny or nasty very often, said to her, "No wonder you're so skinny, the way you jitter around the house. You ought to write a diet book and call it *Twitch It Off*."

Her mother was a twitcher all right, and her small eyes were so sharp that sometimes those eyes could sew Gretchen's lips shut with a quick glance.

Sometimes, but not always. Sometimes Gretchen could fire back, not with a sharp glance, since her eyes were soft and blue, but with her quick, sharp tongue. A "little spitfire" is what they called her back in North Dakota. *Spitfire*, because when she was angry, or excited, or disgusted, or happy, or just plain full of energy for reasons probably only God in heaven knew— when she was any of these things, which was most of the time, she talked so fast and hard that the words really did spatter and spark out of her mouth.

Gretchen liked this about herself. Her mother, in her

jittery way, was always telling Gretchen to slow down when she talked, and Gretchen would pretend to try. But when she was alone and talking to herself, she'd practice talking fast, seeing how many words she could say in one breath—but there was no way to talk that fast and count that fast at the same time. What Gretchen was sure of is if you talk fast enough, people will be so busy listening that they won't know what you're thinking.

"Why can't you just be normal?" her mother would say. What a laugh! As if *she* were normal. And what's normal anyhow? Average, that's what normal means. And it's not as if grown-ups will let you be average if you're youngest. If you're not fat, they call you Skinny or Bones. If you're not skinny, they call you Hippo or Tubby. If you're smart, they say you're pushy, and if you're dumb, they call you the family leftovers. If you like people, they say you're always conniving to get your way, but if you like to be alone, they say you think you're too good for everybody.

The way Gretchen saw things, being the baby of the family meant that you looked out for yourself because you were the garbage pail for everybody else's bad feelings. She had figured out that the youngest had to move fast because if something bad happened, you didn't want to be there to get all the blame. So, Gretchen wasn't just quick on her feet, she was quick with her tongue. Usually, this kept her out of trouble, but sometimes her quick tongue was the straw that broke the back of her mother's patience.

But life is life and Gretchen was trying to make the best of it. The farm in North Dakota had been a big lonely place with a half-hour bus ride to school. That was all right. She'd had plenty of time by herself to practice being what she wanted to be. That was the good part. The bad part wasn't just having a twitchy mother who worried more about whether Gretchen's toenails were clean than whether she had happy dreams, and it wasn't just that she got blamed for every little problem that was floating in the air. The real bad part was a creepy older sister who was as tall and twitchy as her mother but had a mean streak as wide as the stripe on a skunk's back.

So far at this new place in Iowa Gretchen had managed to keep out of any really bad scrapes with her older sister, but that was only because her sister had become so interested in boys that she hardly noticed anything that wasn't wearing blue jeans and a cowboy hat or baseball cap and that had a face with pimples and a few wannabe whiskers.

It was after a few days of being mostly alone exploring the haymows and making dolls out of twine and hay that Gretchen woke up with a brainy idea. The idea came to her when she opened her eyes and looked up at the ceiling over her bed: I'm going to learn to cook.

It was a simple and good idea. Cooking is something you can do by yourself and yet when you're finished you have something that other people like. That must be why cooks become cooks in the first place.

Nobody to bother you while you're alone doing what you like to do, and when you're finished, everybody likes you, even though you didn't have to bother spending time with them.

She ran downstairs in her lickety-split way, past the room where her bean-pole lazy sister still lay sleeping and dreaming about boys, down into the kitchen where her mother was putting away the "early breakfast dishes," which were the dishes she and her father ate off at the crack of dawn, when he got up to do chores before going off into the endless rows of corn.

Before Gretchen could announce her wonderful plans, problems hit her in the face. Her mother took one look at her and started spewing words: "Tie your shoelaces, young lady. No, take off those shoes and go change out of those dirty jeans. And look at the T-shirt you're wearing. You look like you've been wrestling pigs in those clothes. Now git and come back looking decent. And did you take a bath last night? I'd hate to see the sheets after you slept in them. And look at that hair. Your ponytail looks more like a cow's tail than anything a young lady would be seen with."

While saying all that, Gretchen's mother had walked around the table three times, taken a clean knife from the table and rewashed it, pushed her hair back from her ears three times, and checked her fingernails twice. Gretchen stared at her. Her cooking idea was starting to flop before she had gotten even halfway to the oven.

"Did you hear me?" said her mother.

"I heard ya," said Gretchen.

She had to pass her sister's room to get back to her own. Jo-Anne. What a name. Jo-Anne. More a Yo-Yo-Anne, the way Gretchen saw her. There she lay, finally starting to wake up. She must have smelled some food, the only thing other than a bolt of lightning that could wake her before noon.

"Breakfast ready?" moaned the old string bean.

"Find out for yourself," said Gretchen.

She slammed the door of her room and looked at herself in the mirror. So she didn't exactly look like she was ready to go to church, with her stringy blond ponytail drooping like a sick goose neck. She hadn't been trying to look dressed up when she went downstairs. She'd gone down there to work, to bake brownies and bread and pies and, maybe for starters, Rice Krispies Treats.

Gretchen knew that the youngest kid had times like this, when the whole stupid world is too busy to get out of the way and let her do something as good and useful as cooking. First the grown-ups made her feel bad about being little and then they stopped her when she tried to grow up. There was nothing fair about it. Nothing!

She thinks I'm dirty, then I'll just clean up, thought Gretchen. She went over to her bed and rubbed her hands on her sheets. She picked up her pillow and rubbed her mouth on it. Then she pulled off her jeans and T-shirt and underpants and threw them into the corner of the closet. She opened her dresser drawer and pulled out clean jeans and a T-shirt. Where were her underpants? No doubt her lazy sister had forgotten to do the wash yesterday. So why not sneak into her room and borrow a pair? She walked back to her sister's room expecting to ask her in the sweetest voice she had, but when she got there she found her sister had rolled over onto her stomach and gone back to sleep. She looked like a slab of bacon. Gretchen tiptoed to the dresser, pulled open the underwear drawer, reached far to the back, and pulled out a pair her sister wouldn't miss.

By the time Gretchen was dressed and into her second fried egg and third strip of bacon, she could hear her sister lugging herself out of bed. Gretchen knew she probably had only a few minutes alone with her mother before her sister would be downstairs. It was time to bring up the cooking idea.

"Mom," she said, "I got this really good idea. I'm gonna cook this summer. I'm gonna learn how to bake bread and stuff like that."

"You what?" said her mother with a twitch of her head.

"I'm gonna cook," she said again.

Why a simple announcement like that should make her mother act like a steer that was about to have its horns sawed off was more than Gretchen could understand. Her mother started rubbing her hands so fast you'd think they were covered with ants, and then she started pacing back and forth in front of the sink.

"Don't be silly," she said.

Gretchen made her case and made it fast. "You don't understand," she said. "I got all these ideas, you see, and Milly back in North Dakota, she's only nine and

she cooks eggs and makes coffee and biscuits and sometimes she does a whole breakfast and she made this
stew and her mom said she was glad she finally got
some help around the kitchen and there ain't nothin
to do here this summer and last year in North Dakota
you let me embroider that one dishcloth and you're
still usin it and cookin shouldn't even cost as much
as embroiderin because you had to buy the thread
and everything and for cookin I wouldn't use anything
that ain't in the house already, so come on, let me,
all right?"

"I told you no," said her mother. Then she stood tall
and stiff with her hands on her hips. "You lay one finger
on the sugar or flour, you get even one bowl dirty, young
lady, and you'll be spending your days in your room. No
cooking."

Her mother ran water in the sink and started washing dishes. "If you like the kitchen so much, why don't
you learn how to wash the dishes so there aren't chunks
of food stuck on them. Look at this," she said, and held
up a cereal bowl that had some cornflakes caked on
the side of it.

"I didn't wash that one," said Gretchen.

"You can say that again," said her mother, and she
scratched at the cornflake with her thumb. Then she
turned to Gretchen in her firm way again. "I'll tell you
what," she said. "You want to feed people, start in the
garden. You can go pick some radishes and then you
can do some weeding. There's plenty of work to do in
the garden."

"If I pull up the radishes, can I cook them?"

"You don't cook radishes. For supper we'll put some of your radishes on the table. That's as good as cooking. Here's a pan to put them in. And put your glasses on so you can see what you're doing out there. Now git."

Gretchen didn't know quite yet what a good idea it would have been to git when her mother said "git." Slowly she put on her glasses and dragged her feet as she moved toward the door with the radish pan, and that was enough time for Jo-Anne to trap her in the kitchen. She came lumbering down the stairs in her long-legged way and charged across the kitchen.

"She took my white cotton underpants!" Jo-Anne screamed, aiming her words at her mother more than at Gretchen.

"What on earth are you talking about?" said their mother.

Jo-Anne turned on Gretchen. "Gimme them, now! They're mine!" She lunged at Gretchen in her big humpy way.

Gretchen wasn't trapped for long. "Mom told me to go pull radishes," she said, and took off with the radish pan. She pulled a kitchen chair behind her and into the doorway as she ran. Her clunky sister jammed one of her big long toes into the chair. She didn't even have enough sense to put shoes on before trying to catch Gretchen. Now she was down on her knees with her knobby elbows on the kitchen chair and her big barefoot toe hurting plenty.

"You little jerk!" she yelled as Gretchen swung open the porch screen door and hightailed it across the lawn.

"I'm not going to have any fighting over somebody's underpants around this house!" shouted their mother, but Jo-Anne was on her feet and in hot pursuit of Gretchen and her cotton underpants.

"Stop it!" their mother yelled, but the flies had already settled back on the screen door and nobody was listening.

Gretchen cut across the lawn and toward the gravel driveway, which she figured should stop her crazy sister in her bare feet. She glanced back to see if her sister would be stupid enough to run on the gravel. She was! At full speed! She looked like a two-legged giraffe with the clumps of uncombed hair sticking up on her head like horns. She was gaining! I'll use this metal radish pan to whack her on the head if I have to, Gretchen thought.

But first, let's see how she does going down this steep ditch. Gretchen jumped off the gravel into the deep grassy ditch. Her sister followed. It was then that Gretchen learned that the problem with being the leader in a chase is that you don't always know where you are going or whether where you are going is a good idea. The one chasing can see what happens. Even in her bare feet, her sister as the chaser had the easy part. The lummox landed right beside Gretchen and almost had her. Gretchen scrambled up the other side of the ditch, her sister's hand almost getting her by the foot. The chase wasn't over. Gretchen ran toward the tomatoes, then danced and tiptoed her way into the middle of them.

"Better not step on any tomatoes," she said as her sister closed in.

Jo-Anne stopped at the edge of the tomatoes and smiled her big horsey smile, turned, and walked away.

Looks like I won for a change, thought Gretchen. She watched her sister disappear around the side of the house, waited until the mosquitoes started landing on her arms, then made her way to the radishes and started pulling them up and dropping them into her pan. She almost had it level full when suddenly, like a hawk attacking a rabbit that's minding its own business, Jo-Anne struck her from behind, wrapped her big claw fingers around Gretchen's waist and pinned her to the ground. The radish pan went flying and the radishes on their leafy stems fluttered through the air like so many feathers. The radish pan landed under Gretchen's nose with a tinny *thunk*.

Gretchen screamed, "Mom! Mom!"

Jo-Anne held her and said in her cool, sharp voice, "I've got you, you little brat, and I am going to get my underpants back right now. Right now! Do you hear? They're mine!"

"Get your hands off me!" screamed Gretchen. "Let go! You got underwear comin out your ears!"

"They're mine! Mine! Mine! Do you hear?"

Jo-Anne held her little sister to the ground, unbuttoned her jeans, and started yanking them off.

Gretchen gave out the most blood-curdling screams she could, high-pitched siren screams, end-of-the-world wretching screams.

"Mine! Mine!" said her sister, pulling and scraping her way along. With fingernails as long as a witch's! Fingernails that scratched and bit as hard as her stupid, mean, scratchy voice.

Even with all her screaming and wailing, no one was coming to Gretchen's rescue. She felt her jeans slip down and the moist dirt of the garden against her legs—and then her bottom. Her sister had done it! She had actually pulled off the underpants right out here in the garden!

Gretchen pushed her pink-rimmed glasses back up on her nose. She wished they had been broken. That would prove for sure how cruel her sister had been. Through her tears, Gretchen watched Jo-Anne walk away with her underpants. The jeans lay crumpled in a heap beside her. Only now did her mother come out of the house! Now, when it was too late to stop the most horrible thing that a big sister could ever do to her little sister!

Her mother walked halfway to the garden to meet Jo-Anne. She looked at Gretchen where she sat crying in the garden. "I hope you learned your lesson," said her mother. Her very own mother said that. And that's all her very own mother said.

Gretchen stood up screaming, but no one listened. There she stood, holding her jeans, her pink bottom blooming in the morning sunlight for all the cornfields in the world to see. The flies buzzed and the hog yards breathed out their stinky breath. She could feel everything around her—the sky, the clouds, the pigs in the hog lot, the sparrows on the high-line wires—all of them laughing at what had happened to her and how she looked, all of them reminding her that when it came to figuring how much she counted in the world, she added up to nothing.

———————————

THREE

Henry and Gretchen
Lick Their Wounds

BACK AT HENRY'S HOUSE, the day moved along to a supper table that didn't have much talk about La Fama candy bars. Henry sat at his place, "Not hungry." His father sat across the table. The white stripe of forehead below his thick hairline and above his big wiry eyebrows looked like a halo that ended at his temples. He was in no angel-mood, though. His deep eyes glowed under his eyebrows. He looked like there was a little bit of the bear in him, a bear that's wondering whether it was a good idea to come out of hibernation for the summer. He growled a little as he chowed down on the pork chops and fried potatoes. At one end of the table, Granny turned her jowly face from one boy to the next. She looked worried that maybe any second now the lid was going to blow off the table, with everybody yelling at one another.

Henry figured Granny had spilled the beans all right. She'd told his father about the fudge—maybe not about the La Fama candy bar punishment, but about the fudge. Henry knew that it was easy to tell everybody what the youngest kid did wrong because he doesn't dare to fight back. That didn't mean he didn't think about it. At least in his mind he could put the blame where it really belonged. But right now he'd just sit there and take it, hoping that things wouldn't get any worse. Henry figured that Granny only dared to be mean to him because she knew Henry wasn't going to do any complaining. And she probably knew that if she told the truth about the older boys, that they were always picking on Henry, even hurting him so much that his arm was bleeding—if she told the truth about them, they'd argue back so much she'd wish she'd never brought the subject up. Granny's just a chicken, thought Henry. She only dares to pick on the littlest person.

At closing devotions, Henry knew for sure that Granny had told his father about the fudge. He was always reading something from the Bible after supper that was supposed to fit with what had been going on that day. Tonight he raised his big eyebrows and said, "I think we need a Psalm in this house." He worked his tongue around in his mouth for a minute. "No. No," he said very seriously. "I believe I will read a passage from Proverbs. Everybody through eating?"

He didn't look up, but all the boys, and Granny, sat up straight and folded their hands on their laps. " *'A soft answer turneth away wrath,'* " he read, " *'but grievous words stir up anger.'* "

He stopped and took a deep breath. He was letting that sink in. Henry knew those "grievous words" had to be bad. They had to be about him. They had to have something to do with calling his brothers buzzards. "A soft answer"? That couldn't be old spitball Granny the way she had carried on. Maybe the way his father was reading the Bible was supposed to be the soft answer. His father growled again, this time clearing his throat. He read on and Henry didn't hear anything in particular for a while, but then a few words popped out again: " *'A merry heart maketh a cheerful countenance.'* "

The "merry heart" part made Henry think that maybe his father was putting a close to the bad things that had just happened. But then these awful words: " *'He that is greedy of gain troubleth his own house.'* "

The "greedy of gain" part had to be about taking the fudge, and the "troubleth his own house" must have been what Henry was supposed to have done to everybody. Why didn't anybody care about all the "troubleth" he got into trying to get those pieces of fudge to come out even?

The rest of what his father read didn't make much sense. When he closed the Bible, Henry hoped that at least the closing prayer would go easy on him.

"Merciful Father," his father prayed, "we ask that Thou wilt bless this food unto our unworthy bodies and that Thou wilt bless the reading of Thy holy Word unto our sinful hearts. In the name of the One who is the bread of life, the fount of every blessing, Amen."

If Henry had been singled out in there, he had missed it. Henry mumbled along with his older brothers, "Lord, we thank Thee for this food, for Jesus' sake, Amen," and supper was over.

Henry's job after supper was to carry the garbage pail out to the pigs. This suited him fine, especially tonight, when he couldn't wait to get away from the house and be by himself for a while. The pigs came running to the fence at the sight of Henry. One thing he could say for the pigs: They appreciated him, aiming their wet snouts up at him and looking at him from under their ears. "Good pigs, good pigs," he said, and flung them the goodies of leftover oatmeal, eggshells, banana peels, and what have you. Buster was there, sniffing Henry's hand. "Here, Bus," he said, and gave the dog a piece of pork chop fat that he'd saved for him.

The *lup-lupping* of the pigs at the garbage and *gurgle-cooing* of the pigeons in the cupola of the hog house was the kind of music that Henry was ready for. Buster finished his snack and licked Henry's empty hand, as if trying to lead him off for a walk. "Sure, Bussy," Henry said, and started strolling off toward the grove with the dog at his side. Swallows swooped down in front of them for gnats they might be flushing from the grass, then swirled away as Henry and Buster entered the grove, walked past the play farm and onto the gravel road. Henry turned the garbage pail over and sat down on it, facing the west and the sun that was starting to fall in a big orange dome over the distant farm buildings whose dark outlines cut into the sky. Buster sat down beside him, his attention aimed at the ditch and anything that might be stirring there.

Two mourning doves sat on a telephone wire a little ways off, cooing their sad, sweet songs into the evening air. A meadowlark sang its crisp *wee-do-week* from a neighbor's pasture, and Henry swayed back and forth in the sweet world of daydreams.

Out in the corn and alfalfa country where Henry lived, all roads were straight. Every mile was a "mile road." Laid in a square, four roads made a section. A quarter of a mile to his right was a crossroads. If you turned right and drove a mile, you came to a stop sign and the highway that led to Dutch Center. If you went straight ahead through the intersection, in a quarter mile you would come to the old couple's little farm. They were supposed to be crazy and nobody went over there, except in the winter to make sure they weren't freezing or starving to death. If you turned left at the intersection, in a little less than a half mile you would come to the farm where the new family from North Dakota had just moved.

On that farm Gretchen was licking the wounds of her bad day. After having her sister's underpants torn off her as if she were a jackrabbit being skinned alive, Gretchen had sat with her bare bottom in the garden for a while so her sister and mother would be good and embarrassed by the sight of her. She had glanced toward the house now and then to see if they were looking out the kitchen window and about to take pity on her by bringing her some underwear and maybe some chocolate-chip cookies to cheer her up.

They hadn't watched. They didn't care. They made Gretchen feel like the runt dog that can be dumped off along the road and nobody will miss him. But Gretchen decided for herself what to do with what was left of her life after everybody else had dumped her. She was going to end it. She was going to starve herself to death.

She had gotten up from the garden, pulled on her jeans, and sneaked in the back door and upstairs to her room, where she lay down on her bed and prepared to die. She lay so quiet that they'd have to start worrying about her. But no one called her for noon dinner. Maybe they figured they could starve her into forgiving them for the terrible thing they had done to her. Slim chance. She'd beat them at that game by starving herself. She heard her stomach growl. This starving business shouldn't take as long as she thought it might. She folded her hands on her stomach and prepared to die. Maybe just before her last breath, while she still had the strength, she'd sit up in bed and write out a will giving all of her old underwear to her stupid sister.

When she woke up and stared at the ceiling, she thought she had gone to heaven, but then saw it was only her new room on the new farm in Iowa. She started to sit up slowly to see if she still had the energy to do it. She did. It was easy, almost easier than if she had just eaten. The daisy clock on her dresser said six o'clock. She had slept the afternoon away trying to starve herself to death.

She heard her father coming in after a day of cultivating corn and doing his chores of milking the cows and feeding the pigs. At least she had gotten by with not doing her own chores. She heard the heavy squeaking sound of cream cans sliding into the big refrigerator on the porch. That was her sister's job, and hearing those sounds meant that her sister, the real cause of all of today's problems, was in the house too. They were all down there. She could hear them talking.

Their voices got quieter. They were talking about her, she was sure of it. She leaned down close to the screen on her bedroom window. She'd catch the sound of their voices going out of the kitchen screen window and up to her bedroom.

Her father was doing most of the talking in the sweet sing-songy voice he used when he was praying or reading the Bible.

She heard her sister laughing. She heard a "Shh" from her mother. They were down there making fun of her. The creeps.

Then she heard her father again, and this time he really was praying. He was saying the Lord's Prayer. They dared to say "Give us this day our daily bread" when she was upstairs starving to death!

Gretchen bolted out of bed and down the stairs. "Havin a good time stuffin your faces while I'm starvin up there feelin so bad all day while you're all havin your whale of a time laughin and talkin about me like I don't count or somethin? Is this what movin over here from North Dakota means, I'm askin ya? You said we was gonna get rich here and I don't even have clean underwear in the morning! It's not fair!"

Gretchen stomped her foot.

Her father rubbed his bald head and smiled. "Darling, darling," he said. He folded his hands and put them under his chin. He tilted his head to the side a little. Gretchen saw the white lines around his eyes, which didn't get suntanned when he squinted while working in the fields. Now he smiled and the white lines around his eyes closed up with suntan. "We mustn't be too hard on ourselves," he said. "Now, we've all had a hard day, haven't we. Why don't you just sit down now and have some supper. See, your mother has saved some."

Gretchen looked at her mother, whose nose twitched, but whose hand quickly moved toward a plateful of food. Gretchen looked at Jo-Anne, who gave her a mean spiky look. Just when some people were starting to treat her the way she was supposed to be treated, there was always Jo-Anne around shooting a jealous look. Some sister. More like a witch-ster.

Being around her family didn't make Gretchen feel any better, but she didn't hold back in her eating. She stuffed herself, shoving the food in so steadily that she really didn't have the chance to tell everybody what she thought of them. After supper her stomach ached. She rinsed her plate and went upstairs to her room, took one quick look in the mirror, then walked to her bed and lay down to let her food settle. She put her hands over her full stomach and felt the ache return. Maybe her food was settling, but things weren't settled between her and her mother and sister. Especially not between her and her sister. This wasn't an ache from too much food. This was an ache from too much sister and mother. She stomped out of bed, put on her glasses, and walked back to the mirror. She studied herself from the side, then straight on. She was not a bad-looking person, and she looked more like her father than like her sister or mother. Except when she looked straight ahead. That thin face. She turned and looked at her back side. This side looked like her mother and sister. These long legs. Maybe she had her mother's and sister's legs, but right now that meant she would use them for walking—out of this house and as far away from them as she could get.

"Goin for a walk," she said as she left the house, and no one stopped her. She headed straight for the dark grove, a place that she hadn't really checked out very much yet. Until now, it had scared her a little. The trees were a lot thicker and bigger than they had been in North Dakota. This grove looked almost big enough to get lost in. That would be just fine. At least nobody would be able to find her—and that would be just as good as starving herself to death. She made her way through the trees, then came to a clearing. Maybe this would be a good place to sit and yell, she thought. Just yell! She kicked the dirt as a way of getting ready to give the leaves a good piece of her mind. But the only yelling she did was a loud "Ouch!" as she stubbed her toe on something hard in the dirt. She pushed her glasses up close to her eyes and looked down at whatever it was that had just hurt her toe. She was ready to give it another kick, when she saw something painted blue. It was part of a toy, but only a part. It looked like a piece of a roof from a dollhouse. A big dollhouse. Maybe she wasn't the first girl to come out to this grove to get away from her sister and mother. She picked up the piece of dollhouse roof, but didn't see the rest of it. Then she saw something shiny. She dug for it, but it turned out to be nothing but an old root-beer bottle.

She cleaned it off and put the opening to her lips. She blew until she got a sound. She made several quick *whooing* sounds. This was as good as yelling. She blew hard. When she stopped, a *whooing* sound came back to her from some tree farther down the long rows that made the grove. It was an owl, she was sure of it. She had gotten an owl to answer her. She walked slowly, taking a few steps and then blowing again, each time making the root-beer bottle sound a little bit more like the owl that was talking to her. The owl answered again and Gretchen walked farther. When she was near the spot where she thought the owl must be *whooing*, she blew again. But this time the owl did not answer back. She knew she must be getting close. Maybe the owl had seen her and was disappointed that it wasn't one of its own kind. Didn't her glasses at least make her look a little bit like an owl? She started feeling disgusted with any owl that didn't have sense enough to know that she wouldn't hurt it. But then she thought, What would I do if I thought I heard somebody talking and then went over there to find out it was just an old owl with a talking bottle? I'd be quiet too.

"All right, Mrs. Owl," she said. "I'm not really an owl. I'm just me, a girl, see? And not even a terribly big one at that."

The owl didn't answer. Gretchen kept walking, swinging her arms slowly to show the owl she wasn't up to anything nasty. She adjusted her glasses again and looked hard at the leaves and branches for a sign of those soft gray feathers or those big owl eyes. The owl wasn't showing. She *whooed* again with her root-beer bottle. Nothing. But as she went on looking up into the trees for the owl, she spied something else. Boards nailed between some of the branches high up in one of the trees. It had to be a treehouse, or what was left of one. It didn't look like a very fussy treehouse, what with the thick gray boards in a criss-crossy arrangement up there. It wasn't the kind of place where you could go with a bunch of kids and your dolls to pretend that you were in a real house. It looked more like a big clumsy perch, a place where you could stand and look around. Maybe you could sit down if you didn't mind letting your legs dangle.

She dropped her whooing bottle and walked around the tree, looking to see how anybody could get up there. The tree didn't have any steps nailed to it, but she saw it had nubs of old branches spaced just right for climbing. A tree with its own ladder. She stared up again. She had never seen a treehouse this high before. Another little ache came to her stomach, but this time it wasn't from food or from her sister and mother. This ache was the heebie-jeebies. "Yikes," she said. This treehouse was halfway to the moon.

And halfway to the moon just might be far enough from her sister and mother to give her a little peace and quiet. She lifted her elbows, took a deep breath, then grabbed the first nub and pulled herself up, then the next. Hand over hand she went, her feet coming down firmly on each new nub as she pressed on. She didn't look down until she had pulled herself up onto a big sturdy plank. She stood up and tested the boards. Somebody had nailed them down good. This was one safe treehouse—but, oh, was it high! The tree rocked slowly in the breeze. Sitting up here was like sitting in a boat, rocking gently on the water. She looked around, and in one turn of her head she saw why this was the perfect spot for a treehouse. The branches in front of her opened up like a big window that gave her a clear view to the east. You could see forever from up here. She looked out for miles and miles, out across the alfalfa and cornfields and pastures and all the different farm buildings and silos looking like little toys in the distance. She could see the telephone wires running along the road a half mile away, and a mile beyond that the telephone wires along the road, and a mile farther a shining glint that must have been a cupola or something on top of one of the barns.

Seeing so far made the farm that was a half mile away look close. On the road near the grove of this farm she could see what looked like two big dogs sitting down and looking toward the sunset behind her. But the longer she looked, the more they didn't look like dogs. Or at least one of them didn't. One of them looked like a person, just sitting there. A little person. Yes, she saw it now, standing up, and the one that still looked like a dog was a dog, a big yellow one, standing up too. The little person had been sitting down on a chair out there. Or maybe not a chair. The little person was picking up whatever she was sitting on. She was carrying it, a bucket or something. Maybe it wasn't even a she. Gretchen tried to see long hair but didn't. Maybe it was a he. But that didn't make sense. A he didn't go sitting on a bucket at the end of a driveway facing the sunset. At least not the kind of little he-people she had ever known.

Just then she heard the *whup whup* sound of the owl flying away. It had been only a few branches away from her, a bit higher than her head and in the next tree. "Thank you, Mrs. Owl," she said. "Thank you for showing me this treehouse."

Gretchen looked down to see if the ground appeared to be any closer. It didn't. She looked again to the east and saw the little person with his bucket and dog disappearing down the driveway of their farm, and while she still felt alone, for the first time that day she felt happy too. She took off her glasses and looked out again, the way she sometimes did when she wanted to see the world looking soft and blurry. Then she put them back on. She was ready to see the world as it really was. She was even ready to see her sister and mother.

She climbed down the tree, looking up instead of down, and found that it was as easy as climbing up. She walked home and went into the house feeling a lot better than when she'd left. The ache in her stomach was gone. From now on, when things got bad around this house, at least she knew she had a place where she could go. "Good night," she said brightly as she walked past the front room, where all three of them had settled down in front of the television.

The air was getting cooler and the breeze that came in through the screen window of her room almost smelled fresh, or at least more like grass and alfalfa than like pig manure. She stopped to lay her glasses down on her dresser, and there on top of it was a stack of clean underwear. She crawled into bed and, for a moment, she felt almost as happy as she had that morning when she woke up wanting to cook. Gretchen was learning that being youngest means you should never expect anything good to happen. Then, when it does, you can feel lucky.

FOUR

They Meet with a Splash

THE DAY HENRY AND GRETCHEN were to meet was
a muggy Saturday, the kind of day when you can't see
any clouds but everything feels like it's covered by a
wet dishcloth. It was a perfect day for swimming at
the sandpit, which is exactly what both of them were
going to do.

In the Iowa community where they lived, what
needed doing for the week had to be done by Saturday
night because on Sunday everybody closed shop. Nothing would be open: no restaurants, no gas stations, no
grocery stores. Sunday was a day for no unnecessary
games or work. Just church and necessary chores. So a
lot of work and pleasure got squeezed into Saturday.
On the farm, mornings were spent cleaning manure
out of the barns and putting fresh straw bedding in the

livestock pens. Afternoons were for shopping and picnics, and especially on hot muggy days like today, for the sandpit.

For Gretchen, this first time at the sandpit meant that her stringy sister would be coming along. Henry was going to be dropped off while his pesky brothers were brought to town for a 4-H weed identification workshop. Those two should be good at identifying weeds, Henry figured. It takes one to know one.

For Henry, being dropped off at the sandpit by himself was about as good as life could get, even though he knew Granny and his father trusted him to be alone at the sandpit for the wrong reasons. They knew how afraid he was of water—ever since he had watched a neighbor stuff a litter of unwanted puppies in a gunny sack and drown them in the creek.

Gretchen knew that her mother would never let her be alone at the swimming pool because she was too much of a daredevil. At least that's what her mother always said, ever since she had to be pulled out of the swimming area of a reservoir in North Dakota because she had tried to walk beyond the ropes where her older sister had gone. That was three years ago, and it hadn't even been her fault that she had walked into the deep water. She had just been following her big sister, which is what a little girl does.

It's not as if Gretchen was going to tag along with her older sister today. As soon as she had a chance to split, she would. Nothing could be more embarrassing than to be seen with that ass-and-a-bean-pole sister of hers. Especially in a bathing suit that made her look like a skinned long-legged chicken or something.

Henry wore his bathing suit under his baggy jeans. This way nobody in the dressing room would get to see him naked. Gretchen wore her bathing suit to the sandpit too, but only because her fussbudget mother thought this was the only way to make sure Gretchen didn't lose her clothes.

The sandpit was an acre of fresh blue water surrounded by cornfields and a picnic area. It was deep in the middle but shallow along the roped-off sandy shore. Henry looked at the kids who were in the roped-off area to gauge how deep the water was. He did know how to dog-paddle a little bit, but you didn't have much of a chance to become a swimmer at home when the only place you could swim was in a stock tank four feet across and two feet deep. Once he figured out how deep the water was, he got in as quickly as he could so people wouldn't notice that his back and legs weren't sun-tanned. He walked up to the ropes in the shallow part, where the water almost came up to his armpits, and leaned back against the ropes so he could face the beach and see who was there. Everybody else here was a town kid, he could tell, because their backs and legs were just as tan as their arms and faces.

Only farm kids had all these suntan lines. It's not as if farm kids didn't spend as much time in the sun, but they wore more clothes to keep themselves from getting scratched up while picking weeds, and from getting covered with pig doo-doo and chicken what have you when they were doing chores. Wearing caps and shirts on the farm made sense, but out here in the middle of all these evenly tanned town kids, Henry knew his suntan lines on his arms and neck could be enough for the town kids to call him a farm hick.

Gretchen had other worries. People were always making fun of North Dakota, so the first thing she did when she got to the sandpit was take a good look at the other girls her age to see what kind of swimsuits they were wearing. She was safe. She checked out their tans too. Nothing that she didn't have. She saw one or two other girls with ponytails and reached back to see if hers was tied as high as theirs. One group of girls her own age were lying on beach towels, but they were all in a giggly cluster and probably could care less about a new kid in the neighborhood. Maybe she wasn't going to make any friends here, but at least she wasn't going to stick out like her knobby-kneed sister.

Gretchen also saw a big pack of boys on the diving board, which was set up on a wooden tower a little ways out. Gretchen wasn't wearing her glasses, but she could see that these boys were older, and you didn't need good eyes to tell what they were looking at. Their noses pointed at her sister, whom Gretchen had already left stranded a ways down the beach. Gretchen expected the boys to laugh at her gangly sister, but they weren't laughing. When she squinted, she could see that these older boys' eyes were so wide and their necks so stiff that they looked more like they'd just seen a princess step off the pages of a fairy-tale book than like they'd seen the teenage witch that her sister really was. Wait until they got to know her.

About then Gretchen rippled into Henry's afternoon at the sandpit. He saw her standing just off the beach, ankle-deep in water, looking around, her eyes squinting as if she was waiting for someone. Who was she? She didn't seem as cocky as the town kids, but she didn't act as scared as a farm kid either. There was something different about her. He thought he'd seen her before, but people look different when they have most of their clothes off. That had to be her big sister a little farther off: she was a lot taller than Gretchen, but they looked so much alike with their blond hair and pretty faces. And those legs! Seeing Gretchen's long legs, Henry figured she could run faster than he could—or faster than any boy their age.

Gretchen didn't see Henry. She saw herself, or imagined seeing herself, as other people must be seeing her, including her big sister, who had just turned in her direction to see what she was up to. Why wasn't her sister minding her own business and getting in the water herself? Big Sis could swim like a pike. She should have been able to, considering all the time she'd wasted at the reservoir in North Dakota. Jo-Anne was probably waiting for Gretchen to make a fool of herself, but so what? Gretchen decided she wasn't just going to swim, she was going to dive. She headed for the dock that ran down the middle of the roped-off shallow end.

Henry watched as she took off full-speed down the dock on her long tan legs. The only strange thing about this girl, and it probably meant that she was a farm kid, was her ponytail, which stuck almost straight up on the top of her head. It looked like the tail of a real pony in horse shows when the tail is tied straight up. It looked just like one of those tails now as this girl came bar-reling down the dock, but Lord Lord, could she run! She came a-burning down the dock *thunk thunk thunk thunk*, but just as she got to the end she tripped at the same time she leaped. She had so much speed that she made it into the air all right, her arms spread out like a bird that could have flown straight off into the hazy sky if she wanted to. Her fine long legs were not stretched out, though. They didn't seem to know what they wanted to do, and by the time they decided to straighten out, it was too late. Her knees hit the water first, and then the rest of her came down on the water like a door slamming. Whoever that fast-running girl was, she had just done a belly flop the likes of which would make sneezing on somebody else's sandwich in front of all of your friends look good.

Gretchen came up right under Henry's nose. She came up talking, "Yeouw! Never done nothin like that before! Yeouw!"

She shook her head and opened her eyes.

Henry looked around to see how many people had noticed. Everybody had. Gretchen shook her head like a dog that has just gotten out of the water.

"Yeouw!" she said again. "I really belly-flopped that time, didn't I? I was just tearin along there and I musta slipped or somethin and *ker-plap!* Did I hit the water or what? Was it loud?"

Henry stared at her. If he had done something like that, he'd be trying to hide his head under the water now, not talking to anyone, especially not a stranger.

Gretchen shook her head again. Then Henry's eyes met hers. There was a sparkle in those eyes that wasn't scary. There was a sparkle that was so friendly it made him want to smile.

"It was quite a splash, I'll tell ya," said Henry. "That had to be a real stinger."

"Yeah, it stung pretty good," said Gretchen. "But not near so much as that one time in North Dakota when we was tobogganin on this long rope behind the tractor goin crazy fast and my dad he's drivin the tractor and he locks one wheel of the tractor and sends the toboggan flyin at the end of the rope like when you crack the whip and I flies off and goes skiddin along the ice on my rump for about a hunnert miles. That stung, I'm tellin ya. This ain't half as bad as that. I can still feel that stingin. I went skiddin a long ways on my rump, you see."

"North Dakota?" said Henry.

"Yeah," she said. "We just moved here from North Dakota."

At that moment Henry realized that this belly-flopping girl with the greatest running legs he'd ever seen was his new neighbor.

"I betcha I know where ya live," he said. "You're only a half mile from my place."

"Yer kiddin me," said Gretchen. "You sure?"

"You got that red barn with them two cupolas and that big white silo and that big hunker of a grove?"

"Wait a minute," she said. "You don't live at that place with that swayback white barn with them two silos and that bunch of them skinny poplar trees along the road, do you?"

"Betcha I do," said Henry.

"Wait a minute," she said. "I seen that place last night. I seen it. I seen it from my treehouse. You was sittin on a bucket or somethin out there at the end of that driveway last night. And a big dog, right?"

"How'd you know that?" he said.

"I seen ya from my treehouse."

"You can see that good from your treehouse?"

"You gotta see this thing, way up so far you can see everything from up there. You didn't know about that treehouse?"

"Never seen it," said Henry. "There was just older boys and one dumb girl used to live there. Never seen that treehouse."

"You gotta see it," she said. "I could show it to you. You wouldn't believe what you can see up there."

Things were moving along pretty fast for Henry. He'd met this girl two minutes ago and now she was inviting him to her treehouse. But he liked her. There was something about her that made him feel comfortable. She made him feel the way Buster seemed to feel when Henry rubbed the dog's ears and Buster relaxed as if nothing in the world could hurt him. This girl was like somebody who wasn't hiding anything and wasn't trying to get anything.

"Got any brothers?" he said.

"Nah," she said. "Just that creepy sister over there."

She pointed toward her sister, who had rolled out a large beach towel and was lying facedown in the sunlight. Teenage boys were coming at her like stray cats to a bowl of fresh milk.

"All them boys look like they sorta like her."

"Wait till they get to know her," said Gretchen. "I got the bottom of the barrel when it comes to sisters I'm tellin ya." She looked back at Henry. "Where are your sisters?"

"Ain't got none," he said. "Just a couple of big brothers. They're a couple of jerks. Your sister ain't nothin compared."

"You youngest?" she said.

"Yeah," he said. "You youngest?"

"Yeah," she said. "Hey, you got a bike?"

"Crummy one," he said. "Hand-me-down."

"Me too," she said. "But maybe we could go for a ride sometime. Tomorrow after church, for instance."

"I ain't supposed to play too much on Sunday," he said, "but I could probably do that. In the afternoon. You know that corner? That's about halfway for both of us."

"Sure," she said. "I ain't supposed to get sweaty playin too hard on Sundays neither. The Lord's Day, you know."

"Yep," said Henry. "We can take it easy."

But this was Saturday and they had come to the sandpit to swim, so they decided to try it. They didn't really have anywhere to go in the shallow roped-off area. When Henry saw how badly Gretchen dog-paddled, he dog-paddled too, a few feet beside her.

Two chubby boys a few feet from them started splashing each other, splashing each other so hard that the water flew into the faces of Henry and Gretchen too. Gretchen stood up and said, "Hey, you guys, what do you think you're doin? Knock it off."

Henry stood up too, and looked at the chubby boys to let them know he was with the girl who said that.

The chubby boys moved off a bit to keep their game to themselves, laughing and splashing away.

"I guess they're just friends havin fun," said Gretchen.

"Yeah," said Henry. He splashed a little water at Gretchen, but not so much as to start a fight. She grinned and splashed a little back. They were telling each other something, a little signal flashing between them just then as they stood waist deep in the cool blue water of the sandpit watching the two fat kids carrying on. The chubby boys didn't look like brothers, but they had found somebody like themselves. Maybe having a fat friend made them feel as if they weren't so fat themselves. Maybe they were like these fat kids going through the world feeling left out from all the fun, until they found somebody who knew how to treat them right too.

FIVE

They Go Past the Intersection

ON SUNDAY AFTERNOONS, when everybody was supposed to be on their best behavior, the only real sin the grown-ups noticed was when some kid bothered them.

Gretchen's twitchy mother used Sunday afternoons to sleep some of the shivers out of her lean body. Her boy-crazy sister spent the afternoon hiding in her room drooling over teenage magazines. Her father sat in the front room studying the Bible and trying to figure out how to become a nicer person. The television was switched off. "Sundays are a day to find peace with God," her father always said. As best Gretchen could tell, in the eyes of her family, she was the biggest disturber-of-the-peace in the world. She was everybody else's Sunday-afternoon nuisance, so nobody asked her any questions when she said she was going for a walk in the grove. Not one of them would have to know that she was really going to go sit in her treehouse and wait until she saw Henry biking off his yard, and then she was going to join him. What her family didn't know wouldn't hurt them—or her.

Henry had no trouble slipping away from his family either. Granny got Sunday afternoons off and stayed in her basement room, probably eating cookies and cake that she wasn't sharing with anybody. His brothers were upstairs playing with the Erector set they wouldn't let him touch. On Sunday afternoons his father got quiet and grumpy and turned into a bear who went back into hibernation in his bedroom. You could hear him rummaging around in there for a while and then he would be quiet for hours. Henry wasn't sure, but he thought his father might be looking at old pictures from when his wife, Henry's mother, was still alive.

When Gretchen saw Henry on his bike, she scrambled down the tree to go meet him at the intersection. Neither of them really had a plan for when they met, so when they did they just said "Hi" and started playing follow-the-leader with their bikes, making big twisty circles through the intersection.

"Your folks know you're gone?" said Gretchen.

"Nope," he said.

"Mine neither."

"I'm not supposed to go past this intersection," said Henry. "Too many trucks barrelin over the hills from both sides."

"Not on Sunday," said the girl. "All the trucks are parked."

"I know it," said the boy.

It was a sunny afternoon, cooler than it had been for the past few days, with a few bright puffy clouds here and there. Gretchen was wearing her glasses, which Henry thought made her look intelligent. She had on blue jeans cut off right above the knee, a light-blue short-sleeved shirt, and black and white tennis shoes and white anklets. A little silver necklace dangled from her neck. Henry wore his newest straw hat with the red band, a clean peach-colored short-sleeved shirt, and blue jeans. He always wore his ankle-high work shoes when he rode his bike because the heel on the work shoes worked better for keeping his foot from slipping off the pedal.

After zigging and zagging around the intersection for a while, bumping each other's back wheels now and then, but never hard, never in a mean way, Gretchen pulled to a stop and lay her bike down. "I wish you was my brother," she said.

"Yeah," Henry said, and laid his bike down.

"We wouldn't pick fights, I bet," she said.

"Nah, I never pick fights," he said.

"Me neither," she said. "Youngest kids never start it. We don't start it, but we're the ones who always get it in the neck if something bad happens. Every time. Every single time." She picked up a small stone and rolled it across her palm with her thumb.

Henry picked up a little stone and threw it at a telephone pole.

"You Catholic?" said Gretchen.

"Am I what?"

"You know, like Catholic Church. If you got so many brothers, I figured maybe you was Catholic. Catholics in North Dakota had all these kids."

"I only got two brothers," he said. "But there ain't no Catholics around here. You Catholic?"

"Nope," she said. "I'm scared of Catholics. My mom says Catholics squeezed all of us out onto the bad land in North Dakota. That's why we come here. Mom says we was going to live with our own kind of folks."

"I ain't never met a Catholic," said Henry. "You move here to get away from Catholics?"

"That and goin broke," she said. "Mom says the crops is so bad in North Dakota you stay there and you go broke. Crops and the sheep."

She picked up a larger stone and threw it at the same telephone pole.

"The sheep?" said Henry.

"We growed this big pile of sheep and they almost made us go broke," she said. "Mom says sheep are the pits."

"My mom's dead," he said.

Gretchen wrinkled her brow and looked hard at him with her blue eyes. "She's not even alive anymore?"

"Died when I was a real little kid. I know for sure I'm the youngest."

"I know for sure I'm youngest too," said Gretchen. "You know that ole willowy sister I got? She come along and then my folks, they wanted to have another one, but none come and none come and then I almost didn't come, but when I did my mom says it was so hard havin me that she couldn't have another one."

She looked at Henry, puzzled. "Who does your cookin if you don't got a mom?"

"Granny," he said. "This old lady, she's my grandma, she lives in the basement and is supposed to cook for us and stuff. She's mean. I don't like her much. Talk about the pits, Granny's the pits."

"I never knew nobody with a dead mother before," she said. "I knew this one kid who didn't have a dad because the tractor blew up when he was fillin it with gas and went runnin after a rat and let the gas keep runnin while he was doin that and the gas run all over the tractor and when this man come back from chasin that rat and stepped onto the tractor and hit the ole starter, *kabloom* and that was it, no dad. But I never knew nobody with a dead mother before. Is it terrible?"

"It's all right," he said. "I'm not starvin or nothin."

And he wasn't. The first thing Gretchen had noticed about him when she came up for air after her belly flop yesterday were his big shoulders. His big shoulders and arms and his bushy eyebrows. Now, seeing him dressed, she realized his arms and shoulders looked even bigger. He wasn't fat, but he was built different from the people in her family. He looked strong enough to carry two five-gallon buckets of milk at one time.

"What's down the road if we go straight ahead here?" she asked, pointing.

"The old couple live down there a ways, but I ain't supposed to go no farther. Too many hills where you can't see what's comin."

"In North Dakota you could go ten miles without a hill—or a corner. Everything's so close together here."

"Out here everything's a mile apart," he said. "Just like you got a intersection every block in town, in the country you got a intersection every mile."

"That's what I mean," she said. "It's so cramped up here."

They stared in the direction of the old couple's place. "So what is this old couple like, anyways?" she said.

"They're weird," said Henry. "Just a weird old couple that people mostly just leave alone. They're kinda poor. And kinda crazy. I ain't supposed to go there."

"How come? They so weird you can't even talk to them?"

"They talk all right and everything, but Dad says there's bad blood there and I mayn't go over there."

Maybe it wasn't fair to call them plumb crazy, Henry told her, but their grown-up son was sent to the county crazy farm after he got back from the army. The old couple were so poor that in the winter the neighbors took turns bringing food over there and checking to make sure they were all right. Henry hadn't seen much of them so far this summer. Now and then their old Chevy went crawling down the road toward town. They only drove it in the summer. You could always spot them going into town at about twenty miles an hour. It was the car that had all the other cars behind it.

But most of the time they stayed home on their little farm, and people let them alone. During the summer they could take care of themselves. Winter was another matter. Last winter Henry had ridden along with

Granny with a basket of food on the front seat of the car. It had been their week to bring food to the old couple, and Henry had noticed what awful food it was that they were bringing: canned cherries, canned tomatoes, canned meat, a bag of flour, brown sugar, and a bag of oatmeal, of all things.

"Couldn't we just ride past once, just bike right on by their place?" said Gretchen. "I'd like to see what kind of place they live at."

"Maybe we better not," said Henry. "Won't your folks miss you if you're gone too long?"

"You kiddin?" she said. "They're glad to be rid of me for a while. They think I'm a troublemaker. They think I talk too much. They say I'm lazy and don't do my share. They say I don't know how to be on time for nothin. They're always sayin my clothes are dirty or that I need a bath or that I gotta brush my teeth."

"Huh. Me too, same story," said Henry. "How about, do they ever say, 'When I was your age'?"

"Oh, yeah, like, 'When I was your age, little girls were seen and not heard' or 'When I was your age, I got my mouth washed out for sayin that.' "

"Yeah," said Henry, "like when they were our age, all they said was 'doo-doo' and 'ca-ca' and 'wee-wee' and 'poo-poo.' "

"Yeah. And 'big job' and 'little job.' "

"How about 'I gotta go "number one" ' or 'I gotta go a great big "number two" '?"

"Yeah, I wonder if kids got really 'number-one-offed' in those days," said Gretchen.

Henry started to giggle.

"Don't make me laugh," said Gretchen. "I got one more. This is a good one. Don't make me laugh. Here goes. Once when my stupid sister lets one go at the supper table and I says, 'Who farted?' Mom gets all riled up and says that the real bad air around there was comin out of my face, and to shut up if I knew what was good for me. 'When I was your age,' she says, 'girls who used barnyard talk had to sleep in the barn,' and then I says, 'Sleepin in the barn probably smells better than it does at this supper table right now.' "

That did it. They were in stitches beyond repair now, and laughed and laughed and laughed until they had run out of laughter, and sat down for a while, tired, relaxed, and the happiest they had been in a long time.

Finally, Henry said in a serious voice, "There a lot of words you mayn't say at your house?"

"We can't say 'hell' or 'damn' because that makes fun of God."

"Me neither," said Henry. "How about 'son of a bitch'?"

"Nope," said Gretchen. "But that's not as bad as if you say 'bitch.' "

"Just the opposite at my house," said Henry. "My dad don't get mad if I say the 's' word if I'm talkin about pigs."

"My mom says I can't say the 's' word until I'm eighteen."

"What if you step in some?" said Henry.

"I can't laugh anymore," said Gretchen as she started laughing again and Henry joined her.

"Laughin so much I'm gettin a side-ache," he said.

This time they calmed down more quickly, and after a while of just sitting there in the warm afternoon sunlight looking out across the knee-high cornfields and feeling good, Gretchen said, "I'm ready to go see the old people's place. That's what I think we oughta do."

"Can't hurt nothin, I guess," said Henry. "Let's do it. Just don't go sayin nothin funny."

"You neither," she said, though she was biting her lip to keep from smiling.

They pedaled steadily down the smooth gravel and then stood to pedal up the steep hill where the old couple lived. When they got to the driveway, there was a surprise that Henry wasn't expecting. The old woman was out in the garden hoeing.

They stopped their bikes. "There's the old lady," said Henry. "Hoein on Sunday. They don't even go to church."

"Look at her hoe," said Gretchen. "Gettin the job done, that don't look so crazy."

"There's the old man too," said Henry.

The old man was kneeling down on his knees next to the old black Chevy that was parked next to their house.

"Looks like he's fixin his car," said Gretchen.

"No, he's lookin to see that there's nothin under it," said Henry. "He always does that. When he's in town he looks under the car when he parks it. Then when he comes back, he gets down and looks under it again before drivin away. It's one of the crazy things he does."

"That ain't so crazy," said Gretchen. "I seen folks in North Dakota so crazy they was howlin and cussin right in church and throwin their arms around. These folks can't be all that crazy. Lots of folks in North Dakota look worse than these here folks—and them's not the craziest ones."

The old woman went on hoeing as Henry and Gretchen watched. She was a stumpy woman, with a short and fat little body, and she wore a long yellowish dress that was shorter in the back so that as she stooped to hoe, the dress rose up in back to show a good part of her thick legs. And then that skinny little hoe handle sticking out from her and chopping at the dirt faster than a cat covering its business in the dirt. She was something to look at.

The old man stood up and looked toward the road. He saw them, and Henry did the only sensible thing he could think of: He waved. The old man waved back, a big sweeping wave, and then he must have said something to the old woman because she stopped hoeing and looked up. She stared for a moment, and then Gretchen waved and the old woman waved back. All this waving was greeting enough for the two to bike on down the driveway and say hello.

The old people's place was a run-down little acreage, with the garden and several apple trees closest to the road. The house was a peeling white two-story building with a lean-to porch on the front. To the right was a red barn that had seen its better days, and straight ahead was a small red chicken coop, and next to it a corncrib with a wagon and a faded old Farmall tractor in its alley. There was a big doghouse that didn't have a dog in it, and right on the edge of the grove was an out-house with a half-moon cut out above the door. Beyond the outhouse and in the grove you could see several pieces of old machinery parked—a two-bottom plow, a disk, a harrow, a grain binder, and an old manure spreader. The grove kept on going beyond the machinery, leafy branches on top and tangled-up bushes and weeds on the bottom. The whole place looked run down and beat up except for the garden.

As they got closer, Henry and Gretchen could see a stub of a cigar sticking out of the corner of the old man's mouth. His face was covered with long stubble whiskers. He had on a striped engineer's cap, a pair of solid blue overalls, and a charcoal-colored long-sleeved shirt.

"Well, well. Well, well," the old man said, and hooked his thumbs inside his overall suspenders. He took a step away from the old car and showed a limp that started in his right hip, which stuck out a little when he stood still. "Quite a ways from home then," he said. He talked loud, loud enough that they'd probably be able to hear him even if they were still at the end of the driveway.

"Not so far," said Henry. "And this here is our new neighbor, just moved over here from North Dakota."

"So," the old man said, and rocked his head and shoulders. "North Dakota."

"Yep," said Gretchen. "North Dakota."

"So," the old man said again. "North Dakota. That's quite a ways."

"Yep," said Gretchen. "That's quite a ways."

"That's an awful long ways for a little girl like you to be going. You come over here in a car then?"

"Yep," said Gretchen. "We come over in a car."

"You musta got tired," said the old man.

"Sure did," said Gretchen. "Ridin in a car makes you tired."

"You mustn't get too tired," said the old man.

"Nope," said the girl. "I didn't get too tired."

"Not good to get too tired," said the old man.

"Nope," said Gretchen. "That ain't good."

The old woman walked up. She had left the hoe behind, but her hands were dirty and her fingers curled as if they were holding the hoe. "So," she said. "Who we got here?"

"I'm your neighbor, remember?" said Henry. "And this here is a girl just moved here from North Dakota."

"North Dakota?" said the old woman. "That's an awful long ways for a little girl like you to be coming. You must be tired."

"Not anymore," said Gretchen.

"You must be awful hungry," said the old woman.

"I didn't come all the way from North Dakota today," said Gretchen. "We been here a few weeks."

"That's good," said the old woman. "You must be awful hungry. North Dakota. Goodness. Come on, I'll fix you something. I got homemade bread."

Henry and Gretchen looked at each other. Gretchen hadn't been talking much, but she was smiling as if she actually wanted to stay here, to go into the old couple's house without any grown-ups around and let the old woman feed them.

"We gotta go home pretty soon," said Gretchen, but she was following the old lady toward the house.

Inside the kitchen, everything looked dark, so dark that you couldn't tell if the place was clean or dirty. There wasn't any linoleum on the floor, but the wood floors glowed a dark wood color that could have been polish or grime so worked in that it shone—dark wood everywhere and greenish wallpaper and pinkish and yellow curtains and an old-fashioned black woodstove next to a green electric one that must have been put in later, and in the corner a short beat-up refrigerator. Black and silver pans hung on the wall by homemade baling wire hooks. On another wall hung two pictures, one of a little girl carrying a bouquet of flowers into her grandmother's house and one of a farm with red barns, a green pasture, and brown and white cows. Near one window was a little yellow stand with a big brown radio on it and a stuffed brown chair next to it. And next to that was an old foot-pedal sewing machine with a little stool. In the middle of the kitchen sat a gray Formica table with shiny metal legs and four metal padded chairs that didn't match.

Gretchen sniffed the air. It didn't smell bad, but it didn't smell like her mother's clean kitchen either. Her mother would be scrubbing this sucker down and painting all the walls bright colors that showed fingerprints.

There were more than sandwiches that the old woman was fixing. There was some kind of bumpy apple cake and strange-shaped cookies that looked like they were meant to be the form of some kind of animals but weren't.

"You two can set yourselves on that side," said the old woman. "My goodness, North Dakota."

"Yah, yah, here we go," said the old man as if he were talking to a whole room full of people. He eased down at one end of the table and put his hand on his hip as if maybe he needed to put it in place. He took his striped engineer's cap off and laid it on the floor next to the chair. Inside were two cigars. The old man kept spare cigars in his cap. He unbuttoned his long-sleeved shirt and rolled up the sleeves to his elbows. Even though it was summer, he had long-sleeved underwear on under the shirt, and that's what you could see now that he had rolled up the sleeves of his shirt.

So maybe these people were a little bit crazy, thought Gretchen. But so what? Normal people could be a lot crazier.

The old woman kept shoving more food on the table. As she walked back and forth from the kitchen counter, Gretchen noticed her feet. She had on one brown shoe and one black one. They weren't even the same style.

"My goodness, you're a skinny one," she said to Gretchen, and gave her shoulder a little pinch.

"You can't feed a heifer just oats," said the old man. "Yah."

What ended up on the table looked like a full meal. Henry and Gretchen waited to see if anybody was going to say grace first. It didn't look like it. This must have been just a snack.

The children dug in, but between bites, Gretchen started talking. "I got a treehouse and I bet I can see your place from up there if I looked this way," she said. "You got a nice place here," she went on. "It's a cozy and sweet kind of place and I like your pictures. That one of the little girl looks like my cousin in North Dakota, and this sandwich is really really really good."

"You're a sweet one," said the old lady. "You're a little hollyhock."

"This one here is a cocklebur," said the old man to Henry. "What you looking so bristly about, boy?"

"They're cute ones, aren't they?" said the old woman. Just then Gretchen noticed that the old woman wasn't eating. She was sitting there with her hands folded, talking and watching. Then she got quiet and stared at the old man so hard it looked as if she was mad at him for something. Maybe for eating so fast. But that wasn't it. The old man put his hand over his mouth like he was yawning. He wasn't yawning. He was taking out his false teeth. Henry and Gretchen saw it happen, saw those false teeth come out of the old man's face, pink and white as a baby pig. The old man closed his hands over them and put them on his lap. The old woman put her hands on her lap too, and they both sat there as if they were going to pray. Maybe they had forgotten and were going to say grace now. Henry and Gretchen put their hands on the table and folded them. But praying is not what they were up to. Then the old couple did it, like kids passing a note to each other in Sunday school. He was passing her the teeth. They had only one pair of false teeth between the two of them and they were taking turns eating and handing the teeth back and forth.

Henry gave a quick look at Gretchen, as if he were asking her, Now what do we do? She gave him a quick panicked look right back. But the old couple didn't show any panic at all, chewing and waiting as if this were the most normal thing in the world.

Henry and Gretchen kept straight faces. They chewed a little slower than usual so they wouldn't get too far ahead of the old couple.

When everyone was finished, nobody said anything about the dentures. The old woman cleared the table and ran a little water over them. Then she gave them to the old man to wear back outside. They looked as if they had lots of agreement about how this teeth arrangement worked.

The old couple seemed sorry to see the children leave. Gretchen had even offered to help with the dishes, but the old woman would hear none of it. "I want you to come back," she said. "Next time we'll have pie. You don't have to do dishes at my house. You just come back again and eat good. Put some flesh on those bones."

As Henry and Gretchen pedaled down the driveway, she said, "You didn't say nothin about them teeth. One pair of chompers between the two of them! I never seen nothin like that in North Dakota, I'll tell ya that."

"Didn't know about them before neither," said Henry.

"Nobody never said nothin about these folks stickin their hand in their face and pullin out them teeth and the next one stuffin them in her face and chewin with them very same chompers?"

"Maybe nobody else knows," he said.

"I thought the old man's face looked kind of caved in when we got there. The old lady had the teeth!"

"Figures," said Henry. "The old lady must have had them in the garden and slipped them to him in the house so he could start eatin first."

"Wonder how they decide who gets to have them first," said Gretchen.

"Probably take turns, don't you think?"

"I suppose," she said. "Now we're talkin like they're normal or something. They're not, you know."

"I know it," said Henry. "Never said they were."

"You gonna tell?"

"Nope. You?"

"No way," she said. "Somethin else I'll tell ya. There weren't no Bible in that kitchen. Not even a little New Testament."

"Don't know about that neither," said Henry.

"You gonna tell your folks we been here?"

"Nope. You?"

"I'm not tellin nobody."

"Me neither," he said.

"Did I hear her say she was gonna have pie for us next time?"

"When's next time?" said Henry.

"Couple days, I guess," said Gretchen. "In North Dakota Wednesday is pie day."

"Wednesday pie day? Ain't never heard that one before," said Henry. "That sounds kinda weird."

"I'm tellin ya," said Gretchen. "Wednesday is pie day."

"All right, if you say so," said Henry. "Wednesday is pie day. See ya Wednesday."

This wasn't about pie. This was about something else, they both knew it. Just exactly what, they weren't sure. Whether or not there would be pie on Wednesday wasn't nearly so important as agreeing that going back to the old couple's house would be a matter just between the two of them. Being youngest, they'd learned a long time ago that if they didn't have a secret life, they wouldn't have a life at all.

SIX

Chompers, Now Honkers

BEFORE HENRY AND GRETCHEN WENT their separate
ways, they didn't exactly compare the stories they
were going to tell at home. They did agree they'd tell
something—but not all. They both had learned to hide
the best part. They knew that to keep a secret you had
to hide it down a blind alley of stories that are only
part of what happened. You didn't want to pretend that
nothing happened. Too much silence was like honey to
a hungry bear, and grown-ups were bound to start paw-
ing around in it. It was best to throw them a few scraps
of the truth to keep them away from the real honey of
what you did.

Henry told about meeting Gretchen at the sandpit and that when he had come upon her riding her

bike Sunday afternoon, he went out to see if she knew where she was going. He said they didn't come back right away because they played follow-the-leader with their bikes. They had ridden a little ways past the intersection and were real careful about watching out for cars and trucks barreling over the hills, but it was Sunday, after all, and the roads were real safe for kids.

Gretchen said she had found a treehouse and had seen somebody riding a bike and that she had ridden out to see who it was and that she found out it was Henry, that boy she met at the sandpit yesterday, and that they had played follow-the-leader with their bikes and taken a little ride, being very careful to watch out for cars.

That had been enough for the grown-ups. Not a word about the old couple, not one "What else did you do?" question.

When Henry and Gretchen returned to the old couple's place on Wednesday, the old woman was wearing her same faded yellow dress, but she had on matching shoes, both brown ones. The old man was fussing around with a bucket near the chicken coop. "Picking up nails," he said. "They keep working theirselves up out of the ground. Lookit, there's another one." He made a limping step toward it and stooped down. He was right. Old rusty nails were working themselves up out of the ground and he had gathered half a bucket full. When the old woman came from the garden and called them to come and eat, everybody headed for the house, the old woman carrying a little bucket half full of strawberries, and the old man limping along with his bucket half full of nails. He stopped next to the pump just outside the front door and emptied the nails next to it. "Iron," he said in his loud voice. "That iron will seep down into the well, and iron's good for your bones."

Gretchen was right about Wednesday being pie day. Rhubarb pie with meringue three inches thick with what looked like little drops of syrup on top.

They sat around the table in the same places as last time. The old woman grunted a little when she cut the pie, slicing into it with a big butcher knife and cutting pieces twice the size of the ones you'd get at home. Slabs of pie that hung over the saucers she put them on. Big shiny chunks of rhubarb dripping out the side.

"Ohm boy," the old man said, and thumbed his worn cigar down into the bib pocket of his overalls. He rolled his sleeves up again so that his long underwear showed from the wrist to the elbow. He laid his cap on the floor. It had only one cigar left in it. "Oh, the life is good!" he boomed.

"Pie like this will put some flesh on the little sparrow," the old woman said, and put the biggest piece in front of Gretchen.

The old woman had the teeth. It must have been her turn to start first.

Just then a strange sound came from upstairs. A soft thunking, almost like a tapping on the floor, then a shuffling, as if someone were crumpling newspaper.

Then the tapping again: *thunk tap, tap tap tap, thunk thunk*.

Henry and Gretchen looked at each other, then at the old couple. They didn't seem to notice.

The old woman sat down and started eating her pie, smacking her lips and rolling her tongue around after every bite. For the first time Gretchen noticed the big brown blotches on her wrists and her long, dirty fingernails.

The thunking sounds started up again, and now there were scratching sounds behind the stairway door.

Gretchen swallowed and blurted out, "What's that goin on upstairs?"

"Oh, them's just the children," said the old woman. "They're sure busy up there today."

The children. Henry and Gretchen let that one sink in for a while. *The children.* Henry focused on the pie, which, for some reason, looked strange to him now. Then he focused on where the pie went when he put it in his mouth. There went the tongue, pushing everything toward the teeth. That tongue was like a scoop shoving corn into the grinder, he imagined. The teeth weren't missing anything that came their way. First the front ones did their work, then the side ones. Funny thing about teeth, you really don't pay much attention to the way they work in there. And the tongue. Funny it doesn't get bit more often. The tongue kept going after everything that needed moving around. It was busy in there. The teeth were like fingernail clippers, and the pieces of crust snapped off like fingernails. Then they got munched up good on their ride from his tongue to his cheeks before coming back again from the cheeks for a second crunching on their way to the middle of his mouth, where his tongue could check out the damage. By the time it got back to his tongue, everything was mixed together and softer than bread dough. And then his tongue would tell him how good everything tasted. He chewed and listened to his teeth doing their work inside his head. He lived safely inside his mind, thinking about his food, until Gretchen blurted out, "You got kids upstairs?" She had stopped eating. "You ain't really got kids up there."

"Ach," said the old man, as if he was signaling the old woman not to say anything.

"They're my children." The old woman chewed her pie, swallowed, and said sweetly, "You may go upstairs and play with them after you finish your pie."

"No, that's all right," said Gretchen. "I don't need to go up there."

"Me neither," said Henry.

"You'd like them, you would," said the old woman. "Just make sure you don't let any of them out. It's not time for them to come out yet."

Henry looked up from his pie. "You got them *locked* up there?" he said. "You got kids *locked* upstairs?"

The old woman handed the teeth to the old man. She showed her gums and chuckled a little. "Got a dozen of those critters," she said. "And we're going to have more if we're lucky."

Gretchen wasn't worried about herself. She knew

she could outrun these old codgers. She could be on her bike quicker than they could switch teeth. But she didn't know about Henry. She had never seen him run.

"I'm not hungry anymore," said Gretchen. Henry noticed what was left on her saucer, but he didn't have the urge to finish it.

The old woman got up and walked to the stair door. "Stop that!" she shouted at the door.

There was a sound from upstairs that didn't sound like children. A fluttering and beating of wings.

"What in thunder do you got up there anyways?" said Gretchen. She was standing up. So was Henry.

"I told you, them's my children," said the old woman. "They must be hungry, poor things."

She opened the stair door. Henry and Gretchen couldn't stop their feet from sidling toward the door, at least to see what they weren't getting into before they ran for their lives. There were geese! A whole waddling flock of them. Big white geese looking down at them!

"You got geese up there!" said Gretchen. "Those are geese, those aren't children."

"They're *my* children," said the old woman.

"Gotta keep those critters out of the garden until we've picked everything they like to eat," said the old man. "Crazy critters."

"Don't you go talking like that," said the old woman. "Come on, you two, they're friendly, they won't peck you. You can go up there and visit them."

Gretchen gave a little giggle of relief. She looked at Henry. "Want to?" she said.

"If you want to," said Henry.

The old woman led the way up. There were newspapers strewn all across the upstairs floor, some pecked
into little pieces, the rest covered with geese droppings.

"Are they the sweetest or what?" said the old woman.
The geese waddled toward her, then pulled back when
Henry and Gretchen stepped toward them.

"They're sckeerdy-cats with strangers," she said.
"Come come," she said to the geese. "Nobody's going
to hurt you."

Gretchen looked around at the walls. Flowered wallpaper. This didn't look like a space made for animals.
"How come you got them up here?" she said.

"Awful winter last year," said the old woman. "My
children almost died in the chicken coop. Poor things.
Started keeping them inside for the cold, and then
when they started getting in the garden, I started keeping them up here in the summer too. Keep them out of
trouble. They like it."

The old woman really did have a way with the geese.
She petted one on top of the head the way you might
pet a dog or a cat. The goose liked it, and others came
waddling over for the same treatment.

"They're my children," she said. "They know I'll take
care of them. Ain't nothing in the world going to hurt
my children."

The geese had settled down now that Henry and
Gretchen had been up there with them for a while. "I'll
get some feed," said the old woman. "You go ahead and
pet them."

The old woman made her way down the stairs and
left Henry and Gretchen with the geese.

"They do look like they got it good up here, don't they?" said Gretchen. She reached out, and a goose let her stroke its head. Henry did the same. In a minute a half dozen geese had waddled up to Henry and Gretchen. One turned its neck to the side, the way a horse does when it wants its neck rubbed. That's exactly what the goose wanted, and Henry and Gretchen took turns stroking its neck.

"It's almost purrin," said Henry. "Lookit those eyes. These geese are like pets. The smell is something, though, ain't it?"

"You can say that again. I can feel it cleaning my nose right up into my forehead," said Gretchen. "Wonder when she's gettin back with the food. I kinda need a break from the smell up here."

"Me too," said Henry.

They walked down the stairs to see what might be keeping the old woman. The stair door was closed, and when they turned the doorknob, the door wouldn't open.

"It's stuck," said Gretchen.

"Lemme," said Henry. He whacked his big shoulder against it.

"It's stuck," said Gretchen.

Henry tried turning the handle. "Ain't stuck," he said. "This sucker is locked." He gave it another good whack with his shoulder. "Hey!" he yelled. "Door's locked!"

Nobody answered. He pounded on the door. Gretchen leaned over him and together they pounded.

"Hey, let us out of here!" shouted Gretchen.

They paused and waited for an answer. Nothing. "Open up this door before I kick it down!" shouted Gretchen. "You can't lock us up like this. Open up or I'll kick this thing down!" She kicked the door. "Both of us," she said, and sat down on the third step with her feet against the door. Henry sat down beside her. "Now!" she said. "Kick!"

Together they kicked, kicked with the heels of their shoes as hard as they could. The door felt solid as cement on their feet, but the sound was like pounding on steel drums. The geese started moving around, flapping their wings and scratching at the newspapers. The brave ones gathered at the top of the stairs and looked down.

Henry and Gretchen stopped to listen if anyone was coming to let them out. All they heard was their own panting, and then Gretchen heard the geese at the top of the stairs.

"Look!" she said.

Being at the bottom of the staircase with walls on either side of the stairs was like being at the bottom of a well looking up. Three of the biggest geese stood at the top of the stairs looking down—and looking much bigger than when Henry and Gretchen were upstairs and stooping down to pet them. The goose beaks looked a lot longer and wider from the bottom, and the necks weaved from side to side like big snakes that were guarding the only opening that was left to them. The goose chests looked bigger too, like white boulders blocking the opening to this dark well they had gotten themselves into.

Henry and Gretchen tried once more to kick open the door, but it wouldn't give. Then they stood up and faced the geese. "Shoo! Get outta here!" shouted Henry. They both waved their arms and shouted at the geese, but the geese were as stubborn as the locked door. One big old gander, the biggest goose of them all, stood in the middle and lifted his wings a little, lifted his wings so they looked like shoulders, then spread those big wings just enough to tell Henry and Gretchen that he wasn't afraid of anything. He pulled his neck back and opened his beak as if he might give out a loud honk like a normal mad goose, but instead he hissed! He stuck his long neck and big head toward them and he hissed!

Gretchen and Henry felt around for something to defend themselves with. The steps were bare. Not even an old newspaper they could roll up and clobber the goose with. "Your big shoes!" said Gretchen. "Let's both take one of your big shoes and whack 'em!"

Henry unlaced his work shoes and gave one to Gretchen. They turned to face the hissing gander with their weapons raised up above their heads. They started up the stairs, one hand on a step and the other holding a shoe. The gander wasn't backing down. He leaned down toward them with his hissy beak, and the other geese around him acted as if they were going to start getting brave too.

Henry and Gretchen stopped a few steps out of reach

of the gander, which was holding his ground, poking its big long neck toward them now, with his beak open and snapping.

"I ain't never been afraid of no goose before," said Henry.

"Me neither," said Gretchen. "That thing is acting like a broody hen. Like a big, stupid broody hen that won't let you touch its eggs. Hah," she said, and stuck the shoe toward the snapping beak. The gander swung his head toward the shoe, but Gretchen jerked it back.

"Let's let him have it!" said Henry.

Henry let go of his shoe with one terrific heave! So did Gretchen. Together they were like a double-barreled shotgun setting off both barrels at once. Henry's weapon nicked the gander's wings and Gretchen's went flying over all the goose heads and hit the wall somewhere upstairs.

The whole gaggle exploded with honking and beating of wings, geese flying and scratching, running into one another and tripping over their own big feet. Henry and Gretchen ran up the stairs. Gretchen went for one of the shoes and Henry for the other. But the big hissing gander came at Henry's hand and grabbed his shoe by its laces before Henry could touch it.

"He took your shoe!" yelled Gretchen. She heaved the other shoe at the big gander, missing it, but sending the rest of the geese into another flapping frenzy. Newspapers and feathers flew through the air.

"I can make it without my shoes!" yelled Henry. "Let's jump out the window!"

The geese scattered as Henry and Gretchen moved toward the window.

"I still got shoes on," said Gretchen. "I'll kick out the screen!"

The big hissing gander acted as if he knew they were trying to escape. He dropped Henry's shoe and came at them with his wings spread and his beak snapping. He swung his long neck at Henry's bottom and got him. "Yeow!" Henry yelled, and swung his hand back. Gretchen kicked. This time the big gander did get both barrels, a whack on the neck from Henry and a kick in the tail feathers from Gretchen. He made a quick fluttering retreat to join the other scared geese across the room.

Now Henry and Gretchen looked out to see where they'd jump. The old man was near the barn, picking up nails.

"We could do it now," said Gretchen. "He'll never catch us! I'll kick out this screen and we can jump down. The bikes are right over there!"

Gretchen pulled up her anklets and swung her leg back as if she were playing kickball. But before she gave the screen all she had, there was a sudden thudding downstairs.

"Listen!" said Henry.

Someone was moving around downstairs. Maybe the old woman had come into the house and was shoving furniture in front of the stair door.

"Get back!" said Gretchen. "We're gettin outta here!"

Just then the stair door opened. "Hello up there." It

was the old woman's voice. "I got food for the children," she said. They heard her coming up the stairs.

"Wait," said Henry. "Maybe we can run past her and down the stairs."

The old woman appeared with a basket of garden scraps and acted as if nothing strange was going on. "Here," she said to the geese, "I got you some food."

"Hey!" said Gretchen. "What did ya think ya was doin, lockin us in up here!"

Henry pulled on his shoes and moved a little in the direction of the stairs. Gretchen was at his elbow.

"What are you talking about?" said the old woman.

"The door is what I'm talkin about," said Gretchen. She edged in the direction Henry was moving. "You locked the door on us."

"Oh, that crazy door," said the old woman. She scattered food on the floor and the geese formed a hungry circle around her. "That old door does that sometimes when you close it from the kitchen," she said.

"Why didn't you come when we pounded and yelled?" said Henry. He started moving for the opening between the old woman and the geese.

"Pounded and yelled?" said the old woman. "Did you need to go to the bathroom?" She went on feeding the geese. She clucked and talked to them. "Poor things. So hungry, aren't you? There, there, Mommy will feed you."

The old woman didn't try to stop Henry and Gretchen as they eased toward the stairs. When they got down to the stair door, they found it was unlocked.

"Maybe we should see how she likes it with the door

locked," Gretchen whispered to Henry when they were back in the kitchen.

"No, better not," he said. "She probably didn't mean for it to lock us in there like that."

"Maybe not," said Gretchen.

The old woman came down the stairs with her empty basket. "Want some more pie now?" she said. "I like it when everybody's eating good."

"Don't think so," said Gretchen.

"Had enough," said Henry. "I gotta go home now."

"Come back soon," the old woman said. "There's always plenty of food."

When they had pedaled to the end of the driveway, Henry and Gretchen stopped and looked back. The old woman was in her garden again and the old man was still picking up nails.

"My knees are still shakin," said Gretchen.

"You were really gonna give that screen a kick, weren't you?" said Henry.

"Better believe it," she said.

"I think I got a blood blister on my butt where that goose got me," said Henry.

"And she said they wouldn't peck us," said Gretchen.

"I know it," said Henry.

They kept looking back at the old couple. "Never know what you can believe from those two, you ask me," said Gretchen. "They're still pretty scary."

"You can say that again," said Henry. "Good grief. Those crazy chompers and now them geese. Wonder what's comin next."

"Let's not think about it," said Gretchen.

"Thinkin might be a good idea," said Henry. "We gotta be ready for anything."

"We're comin back, ain't we?" said Gretchen.

" 'Course," said Henry.

SEVEN

Sixer's Extras

THEY PEDALED TO THE INTERSECTION without talking. Then they stopped. "Ain't never seen the likes of those two in North Dakota, I'll tell ya that," said Gretchen. "Craziest old codgers I ever seen."

"But I was thinkin," said Henry. "Ain't never heard of them really hurtin nobody."

"There's gotta be some reason why your folks don't want you to go over there," said Gretchen.

"Folks bring them food in the winter," said Henry. "Nobody's afraid to go over there in the winter and bring them food." He laid his bike down and retied one of his shoes. "You're scared to go over there, ain't ya?"

"Takes a lot more than that to scare me," said Gretchen.

"Your knees were shakin back there," said Henry.

"That because I had 'em all fired up to kick out that bloomin screen."

"Sure," said Henry.

"That's the truth," said Gretchen. "But you're not the only one who's been thinkin. I been thinkin that maybe if we bring them food, then we won't have nothin to worry about. That's what the grown-ups do, right? They bring them food. My mom says not even dogs bite the hand that feeds them."

"I can bring food," said Henry. "Granny's got so much food stuck in places, I can easy get some food. And if she misses somethin, I'll just say those big-pig brothers of mine took it."

"Me too," said Gretchen. "Jo-Anne eats like a cow. Maybe I'll spill somethin in her room to make sure she gets the blame if somethin's missin."

Two days later Henry and Gretchen returned to the old people's house with their goodies. They knew that getting caught taking fudge and underwear didn't mean you couldn't snitch a few things. It just meant that they hadn't quite figured out when to take what they needed, who to take it from, and how much to take. And they had to make sure it looked like somebody else could just as well have been the one to do the snitching.

A quarter pound of sugar was hidden in Henry's hat. Granny would never miss it. She put more than that in her coffee every day, and even if she did miss some, she knew that Jake and Josh sometimes put sugar in the bottom of their cereal bowls before they poured out the cereal so nobody would know how much sugar they were taking. Gretchen had a half pound of flour in a plastic sack tied to a string around her waist and hidden under her loose shirt. Her mother would never miss this, because she was always so worried that she wouldn't have enough flour that she had about six bags of it, with five bags open at one time. Gretchen had sprinkled just a bit of flour on the sleeve of one of Jo-Anne's shirts just in case her mother did suspect there was a thief in the house trying to do some cookie baking on the sly.

When the old woman saw what the children had brought, she laughed a gummy, toothless laugh, as if maybe she had been part of this plan and they had all gotten away with it together.

"Let me show you where the flour and sugar go," she said to Gretchen. "Put it right there behind the honey."

A big carrot cake sat waiting for Henry and Gretchen on the table.

"Are the geese hungry?" said Henry. He looked around the kitchen for a clock. Not only was there no Bible in the kitchen, there wasn't a clock either.

"They're only a half a cigar down," said the old man.

"A half a what?" said Henry.

Gretchen closed the cupboard door and sat down for carrot cake. The old woman tapped her on the head. "You're a little dandelion," she said.

"Half a cigar," said the old man. "I can smoke a whole cigar before they need to be fed."

"And two teaspoons of honey," said the old woman.

"Two teaspoons of honey?" said Henry.

"The cake's pretty sweet already," said the old

woman. "Maybe you'd like a glass of milk on the side instead." She put in the teeth and started eating her carrot cake.

"She means two cups of tea," said the old man. "Half a cigar and two cups of tea and the geese will be hungry."

"That's how long it takes?" said Henry. "How long is it? I mean, what time do you smoke your cigar and eat the honey?"

Gretchen took a few bites of carrot cake. "What time is it now?" she said.

"What time do you suppose it's getting to be?" said the old woman.

"I gotta watch my time," said Gretchen. "Gotta be home by four o'clock to get eggs."

The old woman lifted her shoulders and eyebrows. She got up and wiped off the teeth. She handed them to the old man.

"Hard to tell what time it is in the summer," said the old man. He was still talking loud as an auctioneer. He put in the teeth and started eating carrot cake.

"You don't know what time it is?" Gretchen said to the old woman.

"We don't have to be anywhere," she said. She poured herself a cup of tea.

"Do you want some honey?" said Gretchen. "I know where it is now, and I could get it for you."

"If you'll get the honey, Sugar, I've got the time," said the old woman.

"Would you rather have sugar?" said Gretchen.

A goose honked from upstairs.

"Sugar doesn't count for the geese, Honey," said the old woman. "Better bring the honey."

"Who's counting?" said Henry.

The old woman spooned some honey into her tea. "One, two," she said.

Another goose honked from upstairs.

"The geese are," said the old man. "Now, you two eat before it's time to feed the geese."

Henry felt his mind close around him as he chewed his last bites of carrot cake. What would it be like never knowing what time it was? he wondered. When was it time to get up or go to bed or have supper or do your chores or go to church? Time to the old couple must have been like a big sheet of ice that you just slide around on, never knowing for sure where you are.

"You coming?" said the old man. He was standing next to the porch door. "Got a surprise for the two of you. Come on."

"You two go," said the old woman. "I'll clean up around here and feed the geese. I think they just said it was time."

The old man shuffled toward the saggy red barn in his funny *ka-bunk, ka-bunk* way of walking and Henry and Gretchen followed, taking little steps so they wouldn't get ahead of him. The inside of the barn smelled like dusty spiderwebs. It smelled like manure that has been dry so long it smells good instead of bad.

"Over here, this way," said the old man.

"Over here" was half the barn, a big long space where the stanchions for milking cows must have been once, back in the old days when the old man could probably still milk cows.

Something moved in the pile of straw in the corner.

"Got her for free at the sale barn this morning," said the old man. "Take care of her and you can have her. Yep."

Henry and Gretchen took soft steps toward the mound of straw. Maybe a kitten? Or a puppy? Maybe a baby rabbit, the kind with the long floppy ears?

It was nothing like that. It was alive, but it was no fuzzy kitten or rabbit. It stood up with its backside toward them and wagged its tail. It was a sheep, a little white lamb.

The old man started shuffling through the straw toward the lamb, making little sucking noises. The lamb answered with a "Ba-a-a," and spun around.

This was not your average lamb. This was a freak lamb, with two extra legs dangling from its chest.

"That there is Sixer," said the old man. "Yesiree. You can keep her here. Just gotta come over and feed her sometimes. Yah yah."

"Is there somethin wrong with it?" said Gretchen. "What in the wide world are them things hangin down there in front? What are those weird things anyhow?"

"Eh-eh-eh-eh," the old man said, sounding like a lamb. "Just a pair of extra legs. They ain't good for much, but they don't seem to hurt her none."

The lamb didn't look mean or anything. But it did look strange. Henry walked up to it. The lamb didn't bolt. It stood there and looked at him, its extra legs dangling over the straw in front of it.

"Got her free, you know," said the old man. "The rest of her's all right, yep. Free for nothing, so you can have her. Come feed her when you can, you see."

Henry and Gretchen stared at the lamb, sizing it up. The lamb didn't move, and acted as if it was being patient with them, giving them a chance to get used to the idea of a couple of extra legs hanging from its chest.

The lamb looked up. The two extra legs reminded Henry of a Raggedy Ann doll's legs.

"Ain't it gonna die with them legs?" said Gretchen. "Ain't them funny things gonna make it sick?"

"Yeah, freaks die," said Henry. "I seen it."

The old man spit some chewed cigar juice in the straw. "Ach," he said. "I seen worse. Those fellas gave her to me free. Maybe they thought she was a goner. But my idea of it is you get them away from the other ones and your freaks don't die so quick. You just come and feed her every couple days, she's gonna be all right."

The lamb looked at Henry and Gretchen sideways, the way lambs look at people. The extra legs looked like dead snakes now, dead snakes with the black hooves being the snake heads.

"You really want us to have this thing?" said Gretchen. "I mean, I ain't never seen nothin quite like this thing before, just a-danglin and a-waggin there."

"Got her for you," said the old man. "Just come by and feed her every couple of days."

The lamb let out a "Baaa." It sounded normal.

"There you go, see?" said the old man. "She thinks you want her already, yah."

"Can't be our fault if it dies," said Henry.

"What if it gets one of them funny legs hooked on somethin?" said Gretchen. "Sheep get somethin stuck in somethin and they just stand there. I seen it in North Dakota. If they get somethin stuck, they just quit tryin and stand there until they're dead. I seen it. This lil critter gets them legs stuck and croaks, that's not our fault, right?"

They kept looking at the lamb. The old man stood behind them, breathing. "They called her Sixer at the sale barn," he said. "Go ahead and pet her. She's a tame one. Ach." The old man adjusted his weight onto his good leg and stood leaning without anything to lean against.

Sixer stood squarely on all four of her good legs, waiting for whatever they were going to do. Now the extra legs reminded Gretchen of her cousin's braids.

Henry held out his hand toward the lamb's nose. He could have touched the extra legs right then.

"Ought to see her run out there in the pasture," said the old man. "Sometimes she acts like maybe them spares can work. Boy, boy. Tries to run on them. Yep. She just falls on her nose then, but it don't hurt her none. Something to see, though."

Sixer sniffed a little toward Henry's hand. "This critter eat oats?" he asked.

"That's what I'm feeding her," said the old man. "I'll go get some so you'll know how much to give her."

With the old man shuffling off to the granary to get some oats, Gretchen and Henry were alone with Sixer.

"You scared?" said Henry.

" 'Course not," said Gretchen. "I seen freaks before. In North Dakota you'd see these dumb sheep get their head stuck in them little square wire things in those hog-type fences. Sheep would pull back once and then just stand there waitin until they was dead."

"That ain't freaky, that's just dumb," said Henry.

"Well, yeah, sure," said Gretchen. "But one time this man come runnin into these one people's house in North Dakota with four fingers missing that had just been sliced off in a hay baler."

"That ain't freaky, that's just a accident," said Henry. "One time we had this little pig was born with two heads. I seen it. It just went *'glk glk,'* like two swallows of air, and it just croaked right like that. That's freaky. And then this one time we had this Holstein calf was born with a head like a buffalo. Great big eyes like this. And them big eyes just rolled right back up in his big head, all white, and that sucker croaked too. I seen my share of freaks, I'm telling you. Nothing scary about this six-legger."

"I ain't scared," said Gretchen. She reached down to touch the freak's black face. "This ain't so freaky. Wait till you get to know my sister."

Gretchen grabbed the lamb, one hand under the chin and one hand on the rump, the way she had been taught to hold a lamb.

"Don't scare her," said Henry.

"I know sheep," she said. Once the lamb felt that it

was secured in front and in back, it didn't try to move. Gretchen was right about sheep giving up once they know they're caught. The lamb stood still, the spare legs wagging in front.

Henry got down on his knees and joined Gretchen close to the lamb's head. Were those extra legs really real? This was something you'd see at the carnival. Henry pushed the thin layer of wool back on the lamb's neck, just above the shoulders where the legs were attached. The skin went right on from the shoulders to the extra legs.

Gretchen lifted the lamb's tail. "He was right about it being a her," she said. "Least she ain't gonna be buckin us in the rump with them horns a buck gets. Maybe extra legs ain't so bad as if she growed horns."

"So you're figurin we're gonna keep it?" said Henry.

"Well, he give her to us," said Gretchen. "And we don't gotta bring her home or nothin. Nobody's business but ours, don't you think?"

"I sure couldn't take it home," said Henry. "My brothers would pester me to death about it if I come home with a freak lamb."

Sixer put her nose up and touched it to Gretchen's nose. She sniffed. Then she turned her head to Henry's face and sniffed. She wriggled her ears. Henry and Gretchen looked at each other.

"She's a pretty nice lamb," said Gretchen. "Sheep don't always like kids like this."

"Yeah," said Henry. He stroked the lamb's smooth forehead. "You like her?" he said.

"She's growin on me a little bit," said Gretchen. "I

don't got no other pets. She's different but she's really sweet. Look how she's lookin at you."

"I kinda like her too," said Henry. "But what if we take care of her and she croaks?"

"These legs ain't so bad," said Gretchen. "We had a lamb once in North Dakota, it had two tails, one regular and one sort of stubby. Dad just cut the extra one off, and that sheep did just fine. That two-tailer ain't what made us almost go broke in North Dakota."

"Think maybe we should cut them legs off? Think that would be all right?"

"I'd hate seein blood on this poor little thing," said Gretchen.

Henry took hold of one of the legs. Gretchen held the other one. The lamb stayed calm.

"She ain't scared of us," said Gretchen. "I think she's takin to us."

"I know it," said Henry. "Maybe because they're extras it wouldn't hurt her much if we cut them things off. Maybe 'zip zip' and they'd be outta here for good."

"That would be somethin," said Gretchen. "With them legs gone, she'd be a perfect little lamb."

"I could bring a real sharp knife next time," said Henry. "And some Band-Aids."

"Sure," said Gretchen. "We could always change our minds. We might think of somethin else before then. We could always change our minds. I don't want to hurt her, but she'd sure feel dumb if she knew how stupid them crazy extra legs look."

The old man came back and watched Henry and Gretchen feed Sixer from their hands. He wasn't one to smile much, but he showed some teeth at the sight of them getting along with Sixer.

"Just come every couple days," he said. "I'll feed her if you can't make it. Yah."

"We'll try to make it," said Henry.

"We'll be here," said Gretchen.

———

EIGHT

Foot Races and
Firecrackers

THE NEXT DAY was the Fourth of July. On the Fourth, the whole community got together for a whopper of a celebration at a place called The Grove. It was a beautiful day, with blue clouds that were thick enough for shade but not thick enough for rain.

The Grove was this big pasture with about twenty granddaddy cottonwood trees left over from the olden days. Most farmers around there had gotten rid of those old cottonwood clunkers years ago, but this one farmer had kept his. Kept the old cottonwoods and didn't turn that big pasture into a cornfield the way most people had done years ago when somebody figured out that you could get the sogginess out of old bottomland pastures with drainage tile. Dry it up, plow it up, and plant corn.

That's what the farmers who had any sense about money had done years ago, but this one farmer, and he had become a poor one, he'd said, "People have got to have a pasture with trees and a curvy creek in it for big picnics."

Now everybody showed how much they appreciated having one big grassy spot with cottonwood trees by paying this farmer a dollar a car to come and celebrate on the Fourth of July. To make room for everybody, the farmer cleared The Grove of cattle and mowed the grass where the softball diamond would be. He cleaned up loose branches and made the pasture as neat as a front room. This was his day, all right. The Fourth of July pasture put his name in the paper. He may not have had as much money as the farmers who planted corn where their pastures had been, but on the Fourth of July he was more popular than the Declaration of Independence.

Henry couldn't wait to show Gretchen around at the big Fourth of July picnic. As soon as his family's car was parked, he zigzagged through the other parked cars and toward the food canteens, getting away from his brothers and looking for her. This would be her first time at The Grove, and it was about as exciting as anyplace. Even better than the sandpit. And he couldn't wait to see her run the girls' foot race.

Gretchen ditched her sister and parents as soon as she got out of her family's car, even though she wasn't sure where she was heading or where to find the canteens where she and Henry were supposed to meet. What she wanted most was to tell Henry that she had a better idea than using a knife on Sixer. But that could wait. First, she'd learn what this big whopper of a picnic was all about.

They had no trouble finding each other. All the other kids their age were with other kids their age, and besides, they had promised that they'd both wear red shirts to make it easy to spot each other in a crowd.

Henry saw her ponytail before he saw her red shirt. Her ponytail and then her glasses.

"Let's go eat," he said. "Cold pop in that canteen and hamburgers over there." The canteens were fresh-lumber stands hammered together for the occasion and set up under the large cottonwoods. Each church group and club had its own canteen.

Gretchen followed him to the booth where they could buy tickets that could be used for any food you wanted to buy. She followed him, a little behind and about six feet to one side. Who would know if they were together or not together? The sack races and three-legged races were starting. They took their bottles of pop and went to watch. They sat together, which meant they sat against trees ten feet apart so they could still see each other when the people between them moved. They watched the silly sack races, but then came the regular foot-running races.

The younger kids at the big picnic tried to act older than they really were, until it came time to sign up for the foot races. Now you wanted to be in the youngest category possible—or, best of all, the oldest in the youngest category possible. Henry said he didn't want to try running this year because he forgot to wear his tennis shoes. "But you do it," he said to Gretchen. "You can beat all those girls even if they are older."

"I better not try actin like no big shot," she said. "I just moved here and I don't know any of them girls. That one in the pink shorts, for instance—she looks pretty fast."

"You'd whip her," said Henry. "Just tell that lady there who you are and how old you are, and go line up."

Gretchen signed up, put her glasses in her glasses case, and stood in the row of girls that was forming along the chalk line. She didn't lean down with one hand on her knee the way the other girls did. She stood there looking nervous, like maybe she wouldn't move when the lady said "Go."

But it was as if the word "Go" whacked Gretchen on the backside, and she was out of there, her glasses case in one hand and her ponytail a-bobbing. Henry hadn't seen her run like this since she ran down the dock at the sandpit. She was moving out ahead of the pack. She didn't even look like she was trying, the way she ran— not a grunt or a strain about her. She made the rest of the girls look like they thought this was the sack race, galumphing along in this big round clump of a pack while Gretchen was lickity-splitting up ahead—way up ahead.

"Who's that little blond streak of lightning?" he heard one man say.

"Whoa-dhoa!" shouted an older boy. "Glad I'm not running against her!"

Gretchen made the other girls look like a bunch of sick wiener dogs chasing a jackrabbit. She made them look like ruptured ducks in a hailstorm is what she did. The nicest feeling Henry got was knowing how right he'd been about somebody. Those were some legs. He knew it the first time he saw them at the sandpit.

Then came the awful feeling. Henry was the only kid clapping and yelling for Gretchen. There were even some boys their age yelling, "Boo! Boo! Boo!" They wanted the little hot shot in the pink shorts to win.

Where were Gretchen's folks? Where was that tall sister of hers? Why weren't they here clapping for her? A couple of nice ladies did clap. A few nice people here and there did smile.

Gretchen put her hands on her knees at the finish line. She looked back smiling. She put her glasses on and looked toward Henry.

Henry looked around to see if his dad or Granny were in the crowd. He looked for his older brothers. Then he zeroed in on Gretchen's smile. If she saw him clapping, if she heard him yelling, the whole stupid sniveling lot of them could go jump in the river. Even if his dad and Granny and stupid older brothers were watching, Henry yelled as hard as he could, "Way to go! Yay! Ya-hoo! Way to go! Yay! Yay! Yay! Wowee!"

First prize was a giant piece of watermelon and a free ticket to the next softball game in town. Gretchen's smile was practically as big as the huge smile of a piece of watermelon. She walked straight to the tree where Henry still cheered, "Yay! Way to cream 'em!"

She handed him the watermelon. Did he take a bite of it right there where everybody could see if they wanted to? You bet he did. A big chin-dripping bite just off center so that she could have the very best dead-center bite. They both knew people were looking at them. That's the way it would have to be. At least there was no sign of Henry's brothers or Gretchen's sister.

But they were to see big sister soon enough. Jo-Anne was lined up for the older-girl race. This time when the lady yelled "Go!" it wasn't so clear who would win. Not for the first three or four steps anyhow. Maybe Gretchen's long-legged sister was just teasing the older girls. Maybe she didn't want to have people booing her the way they booed Gretchen when she passed the finish line in first place. It was hard for Henry to watch Jo-Anne without thinking of Gretchen. They really did look alike, even though they must have been at least six years apart. Only thing different was that when Jo-Anne did turn it on, crossing the finish line with her long hair streaming behind her and the other girls falling back like so many hobbled cows, there wasn't just one boy her age clapping. There were about a hundred.

Henry and Gretchen finished the watermelon and started wandering around The Grove, where more people were arriving by the minute and things kept getting livelier and livelier. Some of the older boys started yelling and throwing watermelon rinds at one another. Then water balloons. The grown-ups moved away from the action of the teenagers, and the younger kids just watched.

"Things are gettin kinda rough," said Gretchen.

"You ain't seen nothin yet," said Henry.

About then the firecrackers started going off. Some of the older boys were showing off, putting firecrackers under tin cans and blowing them sky-high. Then one teenage boy lit a whole pack of firecrackers and threw it at a group of girls, who screamed when the whole pack went off in a *rat-a-ta-tat* racket in the grass.

But those were the small firecrackers. One boy had some M-100 firecrackers that were almost as big as a shotgun shell. When he lit one of these, it made the grass sneeze. Then some of the older boys thought that it would be even more fun to throw an M-100 at a school of minnows swimming in the creek. But that was good for only one *bang*, and what was left of the minnows zipped downstream toward the river.

"I don't like this," said Gretchen. "They're tryin to hurt things now."

"They're just tryin to act big," said Henry. "There's my stupid brothers. Let's get behind that cottonwood or they'll tease us."

It wasn't hard for Gretchen to recognize Jake and Josh. They were big versions of Henry. Except Jake and Josh looked meaner. She saw what Henry meant about them. They really did look like bullies under their big bushy eyebrows.

Then one teenager got the idea that it would be fun to catch one of the little striped-back gophers that were running around the pasture. They'd catch one and tie an M-100 to its tail. They'd light it and let the gopher go. There were so many boys in on the game that some of them stood on the gopher holes so the gophers wouldn't have any place to get away while the others did the chasing and catching.

Henry and Gretchen heard the talk. "They ain't really gonna do that, are they?" said Gretchen.

"They'll never catch one of those little gophers," said Henry. "Those little critters can run fast as a cottontail."

But the older boys' plan was working. Several of them stood on the gopher holes while the others chased a frantic little gopher which seemed to have only brains enough now to know which way home was—but home wasn't there anymore. When one older boy couldn't stoop down fast enough to catch the skittery little gopher, he tried stomping it with his foot.

"Don't kill it, catch it!" yelled another boy.

It was Henry's oldest brother, Jake, who came running with an empty pop case. Josh was there too, running and yelling and trying to fit in with the older boys. Now they were trying to herd the scared gopher into the empty pop case, trying to round it up like a skittish pony into a corral. The stupid plan worked. The little gopher ran into the box and the boys quickly set the box upright. Before the squirrel could scramble out, one of the boys had it in his hand around the middle while its little legs pawed the air as if it thought it could fly.

"What are they going to do?" said Gretchen. "Why are they being mean to that poor little thing?"

"Don't worry, that gopher will get away," said Henry.

A circle quickly formed around the trapped gopher.

Then, as quickly, the circle broke up, and there was the gopher with a lit M-100 tied to its back, scurrying crazily for the freedom of its home. No one was standing on the holes anymore and the gopher ran sparkling through the grass and down a hole. It had barely disappeared when the firecracker exploded. The gopher hole was like the barrel of a shotgun blasting dirt and gopher parts into the air like a sloppy wad of tobacco spit.

There were a few whoops and laughs from the big boys, and then the quick looking around, at one another first, checking to see if everybody thought it was funny, then farther away to see if any grown-ups or girls had seen them. The laughs weren't all real ha-ha fun laughs. Some of the bigger boys backed away, as if maybe they wished they hadn't been part of this. "Geez," one boy said, and got out of there.

Henry looked at Gretchen. He thought he saw an almost-throw-up look on her face. He didn't just feel angry with his brothers. For the first time in his life, he felt ashamed of them. Maybe Gretchen's sister was a creep, but she didn't go blowing up little gophers for fun.

"Where was your sister?" said Henry.

"She was there, didn't ya see her? She was just standin there watchin, probably wishin those boys was tryin to catch her instead."

Henry and Gretchen started walking away, in the direction of the parked cars, where nobody could see them and where they probably wouldn't be able to see anybody else either. "That little gopher wasn't hurtin nothin," said Gretchen.

"I know it," said Henry.

This was hardly the mood Gretchen hoped to be in when she was going to tell Henry about her plan to get rid of Sixer's extra legs without using a knife. They had almost gotten out of sight among the parked cars when this happened.

Henry said, "Lookit."

The old couple was arriving in their old Chevy. You'd have thought the circus was going by the way the older boys looked at them. The car chugged along through the parking area. It was so slow and so old, it was the easiest car of any to spot.

"There they come!" one older boy yelled, and he almost sounded as if they had been waiting for the old couple to get there.

"It's the crazies!" yelled another. It was Henry's brother Jake. "Come on! Come on! Let's go!" he yelled, and led the pack chasing after the old couple's car.

"Now what are they gonna do?" said Gretchen.

"Nothin nice, I betcha," said Henry.

One big clodhopper of a teenager in ankle-high work shoes ran next to the old Chevy, then jumped on the running board and started rocking the car as it trucked along through the grass toward the parking area. The old couple just smiled and waved at everybody who was watching. They really did look crazy with their floppy faces and dumb smiles.

One of the older boys acted as if he was in charge of

parking cars and waved to the old couple to come his way, where there was a space to park. The waving must have made the old man a little bit mixed up, so he stopped the car to size things up. That's when another bunch of older boys caught up with their old Chevy, then looked at one another to see who had an idea of what to do next.

One bigger teenager said, "Put watermelon rinds under the tires and grab the back bumper. Come on!"

Every mean older boy around there seemed to know exactly what this prank was going to be about. There were half a dozen watermelon rinds tucked in front of the back wheels of the old Chevy before the old couple knew what was happening. Then four older boys got down behind the car and grabbed the back bumper.

"Lookit," said Henry. "They're holdin the back bumper so the old couple's car is just going to stand there and spin."

"That ain't gonna work," said Gretchen. "They're gonna fall on their stupid faces."

But things were going well for the mean guys today, and it did work. One older boy waved for the old couple to come to the parking spot he had for them. The old man stepped on the gas, raced the engine the way he always did, and let out the clutch. The car dragged the bumper boys forward a couple of inches before the tires hit the slippery watermelon rinds and started spinning. The old man didn't step on the gas any harder now, he just let the old Chevy stand there spinning slowly to its heart's content.

What Henry and Gretchen saw then were these two

old people sitting in this car looking around as if everything was perfectly okay, looking around as if they were watching the scenery go by. Only thing was, the scenery wasn't going by. The scenery was staying right where it was, just like the car. They looked like the stupidest people in the world.

"Those boys are gonna get caught," said Henry. "Let's get outta here."

Gretchen looked around. The only grown-ups she saw were watching and smiling.

"Nobody's gettin caught for nothin," she said. "What kind of people do you got in these parts anyways?"

Henry and Gretchen watched the old couple being made fools of. They felt their own faces flush. They glanced at each other, embarrassed, as if they were in the car with the old people and everybody was laughing at them too.

NINE

"No Knives, No Blood"

THE NEXT DAY Henry and Gretchen met at the intersection on their way to the old couple's house.

"Guess what I brung?" said Gretchen. "Ponytail ties."

This was her idea of how to get Sixer's extra legs off. "No knives, no blood," she said. "Just slip these ponytail ties up on the extras, and *psst*, in a couple days they'll fall off."

After yesterday at The Grove, anything that wasn't mean or bloody sounded like a good idea to Henry. He and Gretchen had sulked away from the scene of the old couple's car spinning in place. They had waited between the parked cars until they saw their families coming, and then had separated to find their cars.

"Don't bring no knife tomorrow," Gretchen had said. "I got a better idea."

Now her better idea bulged in her pockets. "See these big wads in my pockets? Best idea I ever got. Show ya when we get there."

"Look what I got," said Henry. "Oats." He had what looked like a pillowcase, tied at the top and about a quarter full of oats. He had put this on his bike seat like a cushion.

With their supplies they pedaled straight to the barn and Sixer. Henry watched Gretchen unload her supply of ponytail ties. He couldn't see how they would do the trick. Sixer came trotting over and put her nose to the girl's cheek, then the boy's.

"Didn't ya ever have sheep?" said Gretchen. "Didn't your dad never put them little rubber bands on boy sheep?"

"What for?" he said.

"You're kiddin me?" she said. "You don't know?"

Henry looked puzzled.

"You don't know about them teensy-weensy little rubber-band things they put on little boy sheep so there ain't so much blood like casseratin?" she asked. "Pretty soon they just falls off like rotten cherries."

Henry's bushy eyebrows rose up and the wrinkles on his forehead got deeper and deeper as he thought about this. He blushed. He looked at her ponytail.

"Then how come your hair don't fall off if those things pinch so tight?" he said.

"Hair's different," she said. "You need a scissors to cut hair off. Believe me. Hair's different."

"So are them extra legs," said Henry. "That ain't gonna work."

"Sure it will," said Gretchen. She spread out her supply of rubber-band ties in the straw. Some of them were heftier than others. The hefty ones were her sister's.

"I still don't know how that's gonna work," said Henry.

"We'll just wrap a ponytail tie at the top of the extras, see, and in a couple of days they'll be pinched off. Just like Dad used to casserate lambs in North Dakota. It's gotta work. Same idea."

Gretchen had started out with only two of her own ponytail ties, then decided that she should have a few extras in case one broke or didn't work. Jo-Anne had plenty to spare, and she wasn't even wearing a ponytail anymore now that she was trying to get the boys to look at her by letting her hair fly loose—anything to get the boys to think that she was some wild thing.

"Wanna give Sixer some of the oats ya brought?" said Gretchen. "While she's busy eatin, we'll just slip these babies on. Slick as a whistle, I'm tellin ya. She won't even feel it."

Henry emptied the sack into Sixer's trough. Her little lamb lips went to work, picking up the oats by the handful and pulling them in for a good chewing. Henry rubbed her forehead. "If it wasn't for them dumb legs," he said.

Gretchen stacked ponytail ties in the straw, big ones on one stack, smaller ones right next to it. "Gotta double it to make it tight," she said. "I tried it on my fingers like this."

She showed him. Henry took a rubber tie and slipped it over his index finger. It was as big as a quarter and hung there loose.

"Twist it," said Gretchen. She picked up another and showed him. "Watch how I do it with my hair."

Henry tried it, but twisting the rubber tie made it too tight to slip over two fingers the way she was doing. He looked at her fingers. Maybe they were littler, but they weren't cleaner.

Henry tried again. "If this don't work, we're just gonna have to cut 'em off," he said.

"Don't say that," she said.

They watched the lamb eating. The extra legs swayed as she chewed.

"I'd hate to make our little lamb bleed," she said. "I seen enough blood spurtin out of animals one time or another."

"I guess me too," he said. He touched the legs, then held one. "They're deader'n a door nail," he said. "There probably ain't hardly no blood in these things. Look, it's almost like they're loose."

Gretchen took the other dangling leg. "Sure feels funny," she said. She squeezed it. "It's warm, though," she said. "It's not dead like a tooth or nothin." She gently bent the lamb leg. "Look at that. It's got a knee. You can bend it right here, see?"

Henry bent the leg he was holding. It was like a long strand of taffy just before it gets so hard you can't bend it. The spare legs had their own knees, all right. He put his thumb on the spot where it bent. There was a bone and joint in there, but he couldn't feel any muscle. It was all bone and skin and a little bit of wool. The leg wasn't fighting back. It still felt loose to him, just stuck on to the chest like a rubber sticker dart from a dart gun. He gave it a little tug, but Sixer startled and stopped eating.

"Don't go jerkin," she said. "Just like when somebody goes jerkin on my ponytail and it feels like they're pullin the top of my head off. I'll slip the tie on this one while you're rubbin that one."

He watched her. She knew what she was doing. While he stroked one leg, she opened the doubled rubber tie and slipped it over the tiny hoof. Then she rubbed the wool back as she rolled the band up the leg with her other hand. She moved it up close to the top.

"Switch," said Gretchen, meaning switch sides so she could get the other leg. He understood. Sixer turned her head now, watching them maneuver. She sniffed Henry's hand and he rubbed her black forehead.

And then it was done. The tie bands were on. They petted the lamb and looked around the barn. They were still alone. They stepped back to look at what a fine job they had done together.

"Oh boy, is she gonna be pretty when them legs fall off," said Gretchen. They stared at the legs with their new addition of pink bands at the top. Sixer looked like she was wrapped up as a present. "In a couple of days, Sixer's gonna be normal," said Gretchen.

Henry stood back, smiling, as he imagined it.

"Maybe it'll work," he said.

"That's what I'm tellin ya," said Gretchen. "And we didn't need no help from nobody."

"With them legs gone, maybe we can take turns takin Sixer home," said Henry. "When she's perfect like that, maybe we could join 4-H and raise her for the fair."

"With them legs off, I'll bet she'd be Grand Champion," said Gretchen.

"Think we'll have to change her name?" said Henry.

"Nah," said Gretchen. "Let 'em guess. Lots of pets have weird names."

They stood watching Sixer munching away on the oats, the little pink ponytail ties staying in place and Sixer not seeming to notice.

"They sort of look like earrings, don't they?" said Gretchen.

"I'm feelin better about today than yesterday," said Henry.

"Let's not talk about yesterday," said Gretchen. "I hope the old couple ain't feelin terrible about what happened."

"Maybe they didn't even catch on what those boys were doin," said Henry.

"Let's hope not," said Gretchen.

They went outside to see if the old couple were around.

"Should we tell them about the ponytail ties?" said Henry. "The old man might see them and wonder what's goin on. He might take them off. Let's just tell them what we did."

As they pushed their bikes toward the house, they saw the geese through the upstairs window, looking out—four or five long goose necks sticking up over the windowsill.

"Oh man," said Gretchen. "My folks better not find out I'm comin over here. Look at them geese."

"At least people don't know about their false teeth," he said.

"At least people don't know about Sixer," she said, "but Sixer will be normal by the time anybody gets a look at her."

They knocked on the door. They heard a chair slide across the kitchen floor. Then they heard the old couple walking around inside. When the walking stopped, they saw both faces of the old couple staring through the kitchen window into the porch, and through the porch window toward the spot where they were standing. The old couple stared, as if they didn't recognize the boy and girl who had sat at their kitchen table and watched them switching their false teeth, the very boy and girl who had agreed to take care of Sixer, the very boy and girl they had invited to come back as often as they could.

"What's goin on?" said Gretchen. "How come they're not comin to the door?" She waved. Henry knocked on the door again. Now they heard the old man shuffling toward them.

When he opened the door, Henry and Gretchen both saw it at the same time. The old man looked scared or ashamed, as if he had been caught at something terrible and was having to face up to it for the first time. Henry and Gretchen knew that look, or at least they knew what it felt like to be a person behind that look, since when they were home they both knew what it was like to feel ashamed about a hundred times a day. But what was the old man ashamed of?

"We fed Sixer," said Henry. "And we wanted to tell you somethin else. We put some ponytail ties on Sixer's extras so they're gonna fall off in a couple days."

"Tell them little munchkins to come in," the old woman's voice said from the kitchen.

Henry and Gretchen went inside and sat down at the table. The old couple sat down at their places too, but there was something fishy. They weren't looking at the children the way they usually did, and there was no food around.

Henry and Gretchen were both used to being the first ones to sense when something bad was going on, and Gretchen was used to being the first one to open her mouth when she knew something wasn't right.

"What's goin on?" she blurted out. "I can tell there's somethin wrong, ain't there?"

"Not much to tell, I'll tell you that," said the old woman. "Nobody tell you what we got to tell?"

"Tell us what?" said Gretchen.

"What's to tell, really," said the old woman. "Tell you what. Let him tell you."

The old man sat down and put his hands on his knees. "We hit a little boy yesterday," he said.

"Hit?" said Gretchen. "I'd a liked to hit about a hundred boys yesterday. I'd a liked to stuff a couple of 'em down a gopher hole with a firecracker strapped to their butt, s'cuse my Irish, but that's what I'd a liked to done. I'd a liked to stuff some watermelon peelings down a few throats too, that's what I'd a liked to done."

"Me too," said Henry. "Them boys was buzzards. I never seen the like."

"No, later," said the old man. "When we were leaving The Grove. This little boy, he comes running up behind the car and tries to grab the back bumper. The bumper caught him behind the leg. Broke his leg."

Everyone sat silently for a minute. It made sense that a little boy would try to do what he saw older boys doing earlier. The old Chevy had old-fashioned bumpers that stuck out away from the car. It wasn't hard to picture how it might happen.

"That ain't your fault," said Henry. "Ain't your fault if some little kid tries to act big, tries to be mean to you and everything, and gets what's comin to him."

"We seen what them older boys was doin yesterday," said Gretchen. "We seen it. It ain't your fault somebody gets hurt."

That was not the way the police saw it. The old man had gotten a ticket for negligent driving. They had taken the keys away from him right then and there, as if he were some kind of drunk or something. The sheriff had driven the old couple home and kept their car. Chances were that the old man would never be allowed to drive again.

"You probably couldn't even see that little kid comin," said Gretchen. "Not fair they go blamin you."

Henry had suddenly gotten very quiet. Gretchen looked at him as if she was expecting him to give a little more comfort to the old man. He sat silently, staring at the table, and in a few minutes said he thought it was time for them to go home.

As they pedaled down the road, Henry said, "I'm afraid I know when it happened. When we was between them cars, I heard some yellin, somebody yellin 'Look out! Look out!' Then I heard the old man gun the car—*rrrrr.*"

"What you sayin?" said Gretchen.

"I dunno," said Henry, "but you don't go gunnin a car when somebody yells 'Look out!' You don't gun it. You step on the brake."

"What you sayin?" said Gretchen. "You thinkin the old man gunned the car to get that little boy?"

"I dunno. Sounded like it."

"Couldn't hardly blame him, you ask me," said Gretchen.

"I know it," said Henry. "Maybe the old man just got mad."

"I wouldn't blame him," said Gretchen.

"Me neither," said Henry.

"Hope he don't never get mad at us like that," said Gretchen.

"Me too," said Henry. "We gotta be careful."

"But we gotta take care of Sixer. Sixer's almost all better," said Gretchen. "You wanna go back, don't ya?"

" 'Course," said Henry. "And we're gonna keep bringin stuff, all right?"

" 'Course," said Gretchen. "Those old folks are worse off than we are."

"I know it," said Henry.

———

TEN

A Sore Bottom and a
Sad Mood

IT WAS AN ORDINARY HOT, muggy July morning. The oats were ripening, the corn was tasseling, and the people were sweating. Henry and Gretchen were not going to the old couple's place that day. They were going to let the ponytail ties do their work. Little did they know that a day with Sixer and the old couple would look normal in comparison to what was in store for them at home.

When there was trouble brewing in their families, Henry and Gretchen were like lightning rods that sucked all the bad fiery rage that was flying around and grounded it. They drew all that family lightning toward themselves. They drew it straight down their spines and into the ground, where it could hide in the belly of the earth and nobody would have to look at it. Of course, when you're the lightning rod, you still feel the lightning. You still get burned. No wonder when you're youngest you always have that singed look!

For Gretchen, it was Jo-Anne who started the sparks flying. Over breakfast big Sis got a scolding from their mother. "What did you think you were doing at the Fourth of July picnic, being the only teenage girl to be playing tag with the boys around the parked cars? I saw how those boys grabbed you when they caught you."

Jo-Anne sat at the table staring down, her long stringy hair almost touching her cereal. I wish those boys could see her slimy hair and drizzly face now, thought Gretchen as she watched her mother pacing back and forth around the kitchen putting more and more pressure on Jo-Anne. "Don't you know how to act like a lady?" said their mother. Now she stopped pacing and planted her feet, her back stiff as a board. Here came the clincher: "You are not going swimming at the sandpit or anywhere else in public until there are some clear understandings about your behavior. You're not going anywhere but church until we're clear about a few things. Do you understand?"

Jo-Anne stared at her cereal. Their father sat at the table listening to this. He was staring at Jo-Anne. "Maybe we could talk about this later," he said.

"Talk about it later?" said their mother. "When is later? I say we come to some understandings right now. 'Later.' Everything is always 'later.' "

The room got as quiet as a dark cloud before a storm. Gretchen knew what usually came out of this kind of silence. Any second now all the bad feelings would swing her way and strike.

"Why am I always getting blamed for everything?" said her droopy sister. She squinched her pointy nose like a mean dog. "At least I don't steal. Gretchen steals things from me right and left and nothing ever happens."

"What now?" said their mother. At times like this, one thing Gretchen knew for sure: If anything could change as fast as the weather, it was her mother's attention.

"My ponytail ties," said Jo-Anne. "All of them. She took them all."

What was most unfair about all this is that Jo-Anne never wanted anything that she, Gretchen, the youngest girl, had. That's the only reason Jo-Anne never snitched from her. That didn't make her a better person! If the youngest had something that the oldest wanted, the oldest would snitch too. Probably a lot more often, because the older a person is, the less afraid she is of being punished.

What Gretchen was telling herself is that if you're youngest you have to be nice and so you become a good person, and good people don't cover their tracks. Why should I? she thought. Jo-Anne wasn't using those stupid old ponytail ties at all, so of course I didn't try to hide anything. It was like getting stuff out of somebody's garbage pail. It was like dump-picking, just taking what would have gone to waste otherwise. And those ponytail ties were being put to good use besides, saving Sixer from looking like a barnyard freak instead of the beautiful little lamb that she was meant to be. Taking those ponytail ties was like going to the dump and finding an old bucket and filling that old bucket with fresh water and giving that water to somebody who was dying of thirst. It was exactly like that. And that's how bad a crime this was. How could she feel guilty for that? Why would a person who wasn't guilty cover her tracks? She had already forgotten about all those ponytail ties and had left the ones she didn't use on Sixer in her shorts pockets, where Jo-Anne found them before breakfast.

"They're mine!" screamed big sister now that she saw she had everybody's attention on Gretchen instead of herself. She had been waiting for this moment and threw the ponytail ties on the table. "I found them in the dirty clothes outside her room. And look. They're filthy!"

She threw the evidence on the table.

It was true. When Henry and Gretchen had stacked the ponytail ties in the straw before picking out the right ones for Sixer, the ties must have gotten a little manure on them. But not much. Good grief. Gretchen hadn't even noticed that little bit of manure when she stuffed the ties back in her pocket. But so what! It's not as if she had tried to do something wrong, so of course she hadn't tried to hide anything.

"What on earth were you doing with all those pony-tail ties?" asked Gretchen's mother.

"Nothin," said Gretchen.

"See?" said Jo-Anne. "She's always lying like that. First she steals and then she lies!"

Gretchen felt trapped. Nothing could be worse than letting the cat out of the bag about Sixer. One thing would lead to another, and pretty soon they'd know what was going on at the old couple's house. That could ruin everything. "I was just flippin them around," she said. "I was shootin them at horseflies."

"Shooting ponytail ties at horseflies?" said her mother. She started fidgeting with her hands. She looked worried, as if part of her was hoping that Gretchen was telling the truth.

"And at bumblebees and stuff," said Gretchen. "I shot one at this big old spider that could've bit somebody."

"Listen to her!" said Jo-Anne. "She's making this all up. She's a thief and a liar to boot!"

"Not so!" shouted Gretchen. "That's probably spider guts you saw on them ponytail ties!"

"Stop," said Gretchen's father. "Stop. Don't heap coals on your sin, Gretchen. Just stop."

Every face in the room turned red. Every mouth closed tightly. All eyes looked toward the floor. In Gretchen's family, after her father spoke in this cold level voice, what followed was the dread silence that Gretchen knew would end in a spanking.

The sweat moved across the forehead of Gretchen's father like the first drops of rain on a windshield. "You need a spanking this time," he said. But he didn't even look at Gretchen, and he left the spanking to her mother.

He walked out of the house, saying he had to get at the field work. He was acting like Pilot in the Bible story, washing his hands and leaving an innocent person to be crucified, this time by a jittery mother and lamebrain sister.

It actually would have been better if her dad had done the spanking. He knew how strong he was and would hold back. Hold back a lot. But her mom, her skinny-armed mom, she didn't know her own strength, so she whacked away as if she thought her hand was like a feather. It was more like a bullwhip. At least Gretchen twisted a little bit for one of the whacks, and her mom came down with the side of her hand against Gretchen's hipbone. That broke a vessel or something in her mom's hand, and she had to walk around with ice on this big blue bulge on her wrist. That should have proved something about who was right about this one.

But then, would you believe it, big Sis dared to walk right into the front room where Gretchen was lying there in her misery and say, "Are you all right?" as if she meant it.

Gretchen flipped herself over, so her face was in the crack where the cushion meets the back of the sofa, and sob-yelled good and loud, "No!"

Then big Sis went to the piano and started playing softly as if this was going to make Gretchen feel better. First, oh so softly, "I Come to the Garden Alone," and then oh so even more softly, "Sweet Hour of Prayer," with a fancy "Amen" at the end. What a jerk.

Gretchen thought about starving herself to death, but that hadn't panned out the last time. Gretchen knew what Henry knew, and that is that when you're youngest you're always the one who "gets over it" first. Sure, you're the one who loses your temper the quickest, but you're also the first one who forgets that anything bad really happened. Truth is, when you're youngest, you know you're behind everyone from the start and that you'll always be hurrying up the rest of your life trying to catch up, and that's why you don't want to waste too much of your life being mad.

Meanwhile on this awful day, Henry was having his own terrible morning. Granny was in a bad mood because some sewage had backed up in the basement, right in the middle of her little sewing room. Jake had gotten the blame for that because he had used pages from a magazine when the toilet paper ran out. "The bathroom isn't an outhouse!" his father said to him in his dark, scary voice. Then Josh got in a bad mood because one of his socks had a hole in it and Granny said she had better things to do than mend his sock in that stinky basement where she had all her sewing stuff. "As if the smell of the hog yards weren't bad enough," Granny said. Then their father got angry at the older boys because they hadn't been spending enough time with their 4-H baby beef calves, getting them ready for the fair that was only a few weeks away. "How do you expect to show those calves when you haven't trimmed their heads and tails? And do those animals even know what a curry comb feels like? And how do you expect to go into the show ring when you've hardly taught them how to lead?"

Henry could tell by how tense their father's voice was

getting that he was really burning. The older boys had been spending too much time on the play farm when the real farm work needed doing. "Now get halters on those calves and get them out there where we can trim their heads and tails," their father told them.

Henry knew you didn't want to talk back to their father when he was in one of his moods, but Jake did. He said, "But it's going to be too hot out for that."

The madder their father got, the more his cheeks moved without his mouth opening. It was as if there was air building up inside his face, and then, sure enough, in a little while his face exploded like a paper bag popping: "Enough!" he shouted, and pounded his fist on the Bible from which he had just read for family devotions. With his fist on the Bible and his big eyebrows bristling, he really did look like he had enough power to bring lightning down upon all of his disobedient children with one hefty end-it-all bolt.

So far everybody's bad moods hadn't turned on Henry, but he knew it would be a good idea to get out of that house. When he went outside, Buster greeted him with his usual jumping and licking. These hot days of July were supposed to be called dog days, when dogs got mean and dangerous, but from the looks of things, Buster was the only one you could count on around there to be in a good mood.

Spending some time with Buster would be a good way to keep out of the danger zone of everybody's grumpiness. First, they walked through the grove, which was rich in rabbit scent, and then along the edge of the oats field, where Buster sometimes flushed those beautiful cock pheasants. But it was hot out, even this early in the day, and they found themselves walking along the shady side of the hog house, where Buster could slurp from the pig fountain and where Henry could run a little cool water from the hydrant and get a drink too.

When he heard his father and brothers getting the baby beef calves out of the yard, he decided to go inside the hog house and watch through the window. It was cooler in there, and he'd be able to watch without being seen. This seemed like a good and safe thing to be doing right now.

His father and brothers had the calves haltered and next to the fence. These animals weren't really calves, they were fat, grown steers, but that's what people called them—baby beef calves, of all things. His father was teaching his brothers how to shave the foreheads and tails of these fat Herefords. He was showing them different currying designs to put on the animal's flanks. He was teaching them how to use the show-stick so the calves would stand the way they were supposed to in the ring.

It looked so easy from where Henry stood, and yet his father had to show his brothers over and over again how to do the easiest things. They just couldn't get the right angle with the clippers to trim the hair that grew around the spot where the calves' horns had been sawed off. They had the wrong twist when they tried to make designs with the curry comb on the calves' flanks. And they didn't have the foggiest idea of how hard or gently to tap the calves' feet to make them get some space between their legs and stand the way they should for the show ring. How can anybody from my very own family be as stupid as my brothers? Henry wondered.

Buster curled up in the straw with his head on his paws and waited while Henry watched his father try and try again to get his brothers to do things right with those 4-H calves. It got so Henry could see the mistakes his brothers were going to make before they even made them. "No, not like that," he'd say to himself, and Buster would look up as if maybe he had done something wrong. "Poke the foot of that calf right between his hoof-toes," he'd say, and then he'd watch his father point to the very spot where he, the youngest boy, who had never trained a calf, knew the show-stick should have tapped the animal.

Henry watched until he couldn't stand it, and then he went out to show his brothers what they were doing wrong. He knew he'd have to be careful. He didn't want to put them in an even worse mood by showing them how stupid they were. He'd go easy.

They were still making the same mistakes over and over with the curry comb and show-stick as Henry walked up.

"Want me to hold that halter for you while you do that?" he said to Josh.

"Let him hold the halter," said their father.

"Don't jerk it," said Jake. "That's Spikey and he's a pretty wild one."

"I ain't gonna jerk it," said Henry.

What he was planning to do was hold the halter chain with one hand, and with the other hand he would do a little demonstrating of how to use the curry comb on the calf's neck hair. So long as he was holding the halter chain with one hand and casually currying with the other, he wouldn't look like he was trying to show off. That didn't mean that his father and older brothers wouldn't have to notice how easy he made it look to use the curry comb. He'd show them how to twist the curry comb and get those nice little curlicues in the calf's hair.

If it hadn't been for Buster, that pretty wild fifteen-hundred-pound Spikey would probably still be running through the cornfields of Iowa. Henry didn't mean to jerk the chain. At the same time he didn't mean to dig the curry comb teeth into Spikey's neck quite as hard as he did. Who would have thought an animal that size would be such a sissy that it would jump almost five heavy feet straight up just from a little accidental sharp jerk on its jaw and an accidental jab of the curry comb teeth into its neck?

"You done it!" shouted Jake, but Spikey was already a grunting one-calf stampede headed straight for the cornfield. The situation had gotten bad so quick that nobody had time to yell at Henry. Henry looked at his empty hand, where the halter chain should have been. He looked at the curry comb and the tuft of Hereford hair that crazy Spikey had left behind. Spikey was a-thumping and a-snorting out of there with everybody chasing behind.

Nobody had ever said Buster was a great dog. They tried to make him sound like more than he was by calling him a Great Dane. He wasn't. He was your standard little-bit-of-everything. A short-haired, yellow-and-white big dog with a nose like a Labrador's, ears like a Shepherd's, chest like a Collie's, and big paws like a Great Dane's. He was your standard farm dog. He may not even have been very smart, but he knew a few things. And he knew these things well. He knew cattle weren't supposed to walk through open gates. He knew cattle didn't go in the cornfields, at least not without a fight. And he knew that you don't change the mind of a galloping steer by biting at its heels. You go for the head, for the nose if necessary, anything to let it know it is going in the wrong direction. That's what Buster knew. But Buster also knew that there was something about this chase that wasn't all work. That dangling chain made this operation a little bit different. It was like the rope the boys dragged through the straw like a snake so that Buster would pounce on it and catch it. Part of this chase was a game of catching that dangling something that looked and acted an awful lot like a snake-rope.

"Get the lasso!" shouted the boys' father. "Get him, Buster! Head him off!"

The father and two older sons were yelling and chasing. Henry could tell by the way they were acting that they expected the worst. A lost calf. A dead calf. A calf too beat up to go to the fair. But it was a crazy screaming chase for only a few seconds. Buster had things under control before they even knew it. Probably before

Buster even knew it. Buster went for Spikey's nose and in mid-jump changed over to the game of grabbing the dangling chain. He brought Spikey to a standstill before the calf had broken two stalks of corn.

Just like that everybody was heading back toward the spot where Henry stood. Heading back, sweating, wiping their foreheads, and keeping a firm hand on the chain that held Spikey. They weren't saying anything, not yet. Henry decided right then and there that he would never join 4-H, or, if he did, he'd have chickens or pigeons, or something else that's small and has some common sense. Nothing that acted this crazy and got a person in trouble just for trying to be helpful.

Their father was breathing heavily. He stopped and gave out a big sigh. "Just go," he said to Henry. "Just go." His brow was wrinkled and his eyes had pulled back under his eyebrows like a couple of angry crows inside their twiggy nests.

"Yeah, go play the piano," said Jake. "That's all you're good for."

"That stupid steer," said Henry. He looked at Spikey and the mucus that was hanging in strands from its nose.

"Who's stupid?" said Josh.

"No more trouble," said their father. "Just go." He wasn't looking at Henry. He was taking sides and he wasn't even going to let Henry know that what he had done was all right. He must have been able to see that Henry had the right idea with the curry comb and that he had just pushed a little bit too hard before the stupid jumpy steer got used to it.

"Dumb, stupid baby beef calves," said Henry. "I didn't even jerk."

"Who's the jerk?" said Josh.

"Go play your stupid piano," said Jake.

"Just go," said their father.

At least his father could have said it wasn't Henry's fault. But he didn't. He could just as easily have said that, but he didn't.

Henry shuffled along toward the house. Now he was starting to sweat. He took off his straw hat and rubbed his forehead. When he put his hand down, Buster licked at the sweat. He sat down with the dog on the shady north side of the house and leaned back. The day couldn't get any lower than this.

I wonder if Gretchen is having a better day, he thought. I wonder if Sixer's extras have fallen off yet. Back at her house, Gretchen wondered if Henry was having a better day. She wondered if Sixer's extras had fallen off yet. But they had agreed to wait for the pony-tail ties to do their work and definitely were not going over to the old couple's house until a few days had passed. Gretchen decided to take her sore bottom to her treehouse and look at the clouds. Henry decided to take his sad mood for a ride on his bike. Maybe at least the mourning doves would be cooing on this muggy awful day.

ELEVEN

"It Helps to Talk"

HENRY PUMPED HIS BICYCLE slowly down the gravel road toward the intersection. He saw a cloud of dust from the gravel road billowing up in a long golden stream behind a feed truck. It was so easy to spot a truck coming down that road, he wondered why everyone was always so worried about him heading in this direction. From her treehouse, Gretchen saw the same cloud of gravelly dust. She adjusted a couple of small pillows she had brought up to her perch and then looked out through her picture-window opening in the direction of Henry's place. She recognized his straw hat and the way he pedaled. She was afraid he was going by himself to see if Sixer's extra legs had fallen off.

"Hey, we're supposed to wait!" she yelled into the sky, but he was much too far away to hear.

She climbed down and got on her bike. If she hurried, he'd be able to see her when he got to the intersection and she'd be able to stop him from going over to the old couple's house before the ponytail ties had time to take off Sixer's extras. But when she got to the intersection, she saw that Henry had no intention of going any farther. He had parked his bike and was in the ditch picking milkweed pods, breaking them open and blowing on their beautiful ivory-colored layers of seeds, which looked like feathers.

She laid her bike down and walked toward him. He looked up and could see by the slow way she walked that something terrible had happened. She could see that there was something wrong with him too.

"Hi," said Henry. "What a crappy day."

"You too?" she said. "I ain't never had a crappier day."

"Real crappy. Super-duper crappy," he said. He held out the opened milkweed pod and showed her the pretty seeds that lay there like tail feathers of a tiny white ostrich.

"Best thing I seen all day," she said.

"Wanna play follow-the-leader around the intersection?" he said.

"My butt's sore," she said. "My stupid mom whipped me for taking those ponytail ties. My stupid sister started it."

"My stupid brothers got me in trouble too," he said.

They sat down on the edge of the ditch, looking at the intersection where they had first met on their bicycles. It wasn't the same. It wasn't the way it was the first time when they hardly knew each other and when the sunshine felt like the world was made for boys and girls on bicycles, when the sunshine felt sweet and soothing, as if it could put you in a good mood and get you ready to make the best friend of your whole life.

Gretchen started talking, mumbling at first so that Henry couldn't hear what she was saying, and then a little louder as if she had warmed up on something.

"Just when you think things are good, they get bad is what I'm thinkin," she said. "Sixer and you and maybe even the old couple, that's the good part. Makes you forget the rest for a while. Crazy sister and crabby mom and grumpy dad, that's what I got at home," she said.

"I know it," he said. "Same story with me."

"Like today," she said. "I get up and I'm in a good mood, ready to spread a little happiness around, right? That's what I am, a sprinkler of happiness. I'd laugh all day if somebody gave me half a chance."

"Me too," said Henry. "Ain't never my idea to get grumpy. My trouble is, every time I sprinkle anything, I get blamed. Like spillin a couple crumbs on the floor."

"That's what I'm sayin," said Gretchen. "They'll blame you if a drawer is left half open."

"They'll blame you if there's a stinky smell in the bathroom."

"That's what I'm sayin," said Gretchen. "They'll blame you if somebody uses too much air freshener to clean up that stink."

"They'd blame you for fly specks on the window if they could get away with it."

"I always get blamed if somebody gets sick at our house," said Gretchen.

"Me too," said Henry. "They'll blame me for all the colds people catch just because I'm the first one to sneeze."

"Right," said Gretchen. "I wanna tell 'em, 'You'd sneeze first too if everybody above you poured their snotty old germs on your head.' "

"What I'd like to know," said Henry, "is why would cold germs want to go after the littlest kids first anyhow when they've got all those big juicy grown-up noses to crawl up in."

"That's exactly what I'm sayin," said Gretchen. "So, you see, this morning I'm just sittin at the table mindin my own business and B.B. Brain says I took her ponytail ties. Just like that—*ka-pow!* the whole works goes nuts on me."

"You ain't seen nuts until you seen the way my brothers went berserk today. I'm helpin them with their dumb old 4-H calves and one of them scares because they haven't got that calf trained, you see, and takes off like crazy, and I get the blame. Can you believe it?"

"I think people are crazier in Iowa," said Gretchen. "In North Dakota there was so much space people's bad moods didn't have to go bumpin into each other all the time. You could just go outside and swing your arms around all day and you wouldn't hit nothin like somebody else's bad mood. You could sing and fart and do anything you wanted to and you wouldn't go bumpin into somebody's ole sour-pussin moods. Geez."

"Sounds fun," said Henry. "You wanna go back?"

"Sometimes," she said. "I'd go back in a minute if you was my brother. And if we could bring Sixer. Big people are the problem, you ask me."

"I know it," said Henry. "It wouldn't be so bad if people would just shut up and listen to what you're sayin," said Henry.

"Right," said Gretchen. "Most people don't understand. Like my mom and stupid sister. They're always sayin I done these bad things I didn't do. Always pickin and always pickin."

"Know what you mean," said Henry.

"This one time," said Gretchen, "some of my sister's underwear got mixed up in my drawer and I wore 'em by accident. Just an accident, you know? And when she can't find 'em, she tells Mom, and Mom says to me, 'Let me see what underwear you got on,' and I says, 'Why?' I don't pay attention to that kind of thing, I don't care if I got my sister's underwear on by accident, it's all the same to me. And she says, 'Show me,' and my stupid sister is getting all het-up standin there in her robe because she didn't wash the underwear like she's supposed to, it's her job, and so she's a-pointin and a-yellin and Mom is gettin more riled up because she don't like yellin in the house and so I just leave to get away from the yellin, and they chase after me like I done somethin wrong—well, I ain't done nothin wrong, so I lets them catch me. Why not, I figures, I ain't done nothin wrong after all. So would you believe they grabs me and just tears my clothes off, just rips my jeans to pieces like they was goin crazy—that's my very own mother and my big sister doin this—and I just lays there because, you know, I ain't done nothin wrong and I'm still tryin to figure out what is going on here, you know, I'm thinkin this is keeee-raaaay-zeeee! What is goin on here! And you know I didn't mind havin my clothes all tore to pieces and gettin all scratched up so I'm bleedin all over my back, and all the neighbors have stopped on the road and are seein what's happenin and seein me like that, but what gets my goat real bad is they just don't listen. They wouldn't understand it was just an accident and I didn't do nothin wrong. People just don't listen to ya."

"I'd get even," said Henry. "I'd wait and get even."

"Maybe I will," she said. "Someday I'll figure out some way to get even."

"Granny and my brothers are worse, I'll betcha," said Henry. "This one time Granny made this yucky, sticky fudge she's always makin and eatin most of it herself before anybody else sees it, and this one time she tells me to take a pile of this sticky stuff out to my brothers, she's too lazy to bring it out to 'em herself, she's this big tub—*bah-rgh*—this wide, you know, and I says, okay, and so she hands me a whole pile of this stuff and I'm walkin toward the grove where my brothers are, and all of a sudden, we got this crazy mean rooster that comes after you and flies up at you from behind and scratches you up—"

"Yeah, there was this rooster in North Dakota, he scratched this little kid's eyes out once."

"Yeah, well, this rooster—we call him Freeko—I'm just a-walkin past the chicken coop and all of a sudden

Freeko comes flyin and scratchin from behind and—
wham!—hits me right in the neck, and I falls down with
all that fudge right smack in the dirt, and who knows
what's all in that dirt, you know, so I gets myself up and
I says, 'Oh boy, this is some mess,' and I goes back to
Granny and says, 'Lookit, Freeko knocked me right
down in the dirt.' You know what Granny did?"

"What?" said Gretchen.

"She made me eat it."

Gretchen stood up, startled. "She what!"

"Granny made me eat that dirty, yucky fudge, I said.
I took one bite and puked," said Henry. "Was sick for
a week."

"Yuck!" said Gretchen. "I'd get even."

"I'm gonna," said Henry. "Someday I'm gonna."
Henry stood up. "I'm feelin a lot better," he said.

"Me too," said Gretchen. "It helps to talk, don't it?"

"It sure does," he said. "And it's good to have somebody who listens to ya for a change."

"Say," said Gretchen. "It ain't time for chores yet.
Why don't you bike on over and have a look at my
treehouse—you still ain't seen it. We can leave our
bikes in the grove and sneak right up there without
anybody botherin us."

"I dunno," said Henry. "I don't want no more trouble today."

"Half hour," she said. "Come on."

They biked up to the grove around Gretchen's
farm, laid their bikes in the ditch, and ran through
the grove.

They stood under the treehouse and looked up. Henry had thought it would be something a little closer to the ground, something you could reach up and touch. This wasn't a treehouse, this was a sky house.

"Holy cow!" he said, and just stared. He saw the planks and scraps of lumber sticking out over the branches in the distant perch overhead. To him it looked like one of those high and twiggy crow nests. He walked around the tree a few times, staring up. "Holy cow or what!" he said.

Gretchen saw his red, scared face.

"It ain't so bad once you climbed it a couple times," she said. "See them steps? They're perfect for climbin. Just don't look down."

"I better watch to see how you do it," said Henry. "I ain't got good shoes on for this."

Gretchen looked at his work shoes. They had thick rubber soles that could probably walk straight up a roof.

"You go," she said. "I'll come right behind and put my hand on your foot so you know you won't slip."

Henry felt the world close in around him fast. It's not as if he hadn't had this feeling before, especially with his older brothers, when he'd be cornered into doing something that everything inside him told him he shouldn't be trying. This was worse than the time his brothers challenged him to try milking a first-calf heifer that had never felt a human hand on its udder before. This was worse than the first time he was told to hold a young pig by its hind legs for castrating. It was one of those moments when he felt his insides didn't have anywhere to go, like he'd just been found out for every bad thing he'd done in his whole life. What was different this time was that the other person knew how he felt. He looked at Gretchen and saw somebody who wouldn't laugh at him if after three steps he said he couldn't do it.

"I'll give 'er a try," he said, and took hold of the first branch.

"It ain't scary once you done it," she said, "and oh boy, are you gonna like it up there."

Henry was off the ground and climbing. His legs were shaking like a scared puppy's.

"Just keep goin," she said. "I'll keep your foot on the steps." When she put her hand on his foot, his legs stopped shaking.

She climbed right behind him, putting her hand over his lower foot with each step.

"Don't look down," she said.

His leg started shaking again.

"Sorry," she said.

"It's all right."

They kept climbing. The last few steps, he moved faster, looking up toward the planks that were just above him.

And when they were there, he crawled on his hands and knees, testing the floor. It was sturdy. He stood up and looked around.

Gretchen smiled. "You like it?"

"Never seen nothin like it in my life," he said. "It's not even teetery." He shifted his weight from one foot to the other.

"Wanna see the view?" she asked. "Turn around."

He turned and looked through the great leafy window, the same one through which Gretchen had first seen him. This was the very spot where she had sat and watched him sitting on his bucket at the end of the driveway with Buster.

Henry's lips did not move. He put his hands on his hips. He stared. He put his hands by his sides. He stared. How could the world be so beautiful when only a few hours ago he had been made to feel that people liked him about as much as they liked a dead fly in their milk?

"And ya get more than a view," said Gretchen. "Lookit these cushions I got. They're feed sacks filled with grass. Nice and soft. You don't have to sit on the hump at my place."

Henry knew exactly what she meant. The littlest kids always had to sit on the hump. That's really the long and short of it when you're youngest. You have to sit on the hump, whatever the hump might be. Sometimes it's in the middle of the backseat of the car, but sometimes it's somebody's knee. That's what being youngest is all about: You get the hump. And if there isn't a hump handy, the grown-ups will make one up— like a box to sit on for taking pictures so your head will come up as high as other people's, or it might be some stupid catalog they stick under you when you go to somebody's house and there isn't a kid's chair. This was one place to be the youngest and not have to sit on the hump.

Henry sat down on the grass-clipping cushion. It felt as nice as it looked.

"This is really somethin," he said. He folded his arms and looked out again over the great expanse of farmland. He sat motionless with a little smile on his face.

"You're a thinker, aren't you?" she said.

"When there's somethin to think about," he said.

"So what are you thinkin about?"

He blinked his eyes. He ran his tongue along his lips. "I'm just thinkin," he said.

She sat down next to him. A breeze came up and moved the tree. They sat swaying slowly, like people in a boat on a calm lake. Together they stared out over the miles and miles of farms, the square sections of land stretching out before them like a patchwork of fields threaded in rows of green corn.

"What are ya just thinkin?" she said.

"I'm thinkin," he said. "I'm thinkin this day is turning out a lot better than it started."

"You can say that again," she said.

TWELVE

Sixer in the Sky

IT WAS A COOL, SUNNY DAY as Henry and Gretchen biked toward the old couple's house to see what the ponytail ties had done. Maybe the extras wouldn't be totally off yet, just really loose, like a tooth that you push around in your mouth for a few days before eating an apple or a little yank with a piece of thread does the trick. That wouldn't be so bad.

"Maybe we should bring a piece of thread just in case," Henry had suggested. "We could use it the way you do on a loose tooth—just give the legs a little yank if they ain't quite off."

"Those ponytail ties was so tight," Gretchen said, "them legs either falled off by now or are fixin to fall."

But there was more to think about than just Sixer's extras. "Food and feed," as they put it. They'd bring feed for Sixer, but what better way to make sure the old couple stayed in a good mood than to bring them lots of food too?

"Keep their bellies full of sweet stuff—that should keep 'em from gettin wild on us," said Gretchen. "The way they eat, plenty of food will keep 'em happy."

In their last sweet minutes up in the treehouse the day before, Gretchen and Henry had made a plan. Instead of taking so much food and feed to the old couple's place at one time, they'd build up a stash in the old couple's grove. This way either one of them could sneak food over there when nobody was watching and they'd always have plenty if they needed it.

Gretchen brought more oats for Sixer from the big oats bin on her farm and half a bag of sugar from the basement. "My mom still ain't finished unpacking all the cooking stuff yet," she said. "She'll never miss this sugar. And look. I got somethin else—cinnamon!"

Henry had gone out to Granny's garden and pulled a few potatoes out from under the potato plants. You don't have to dig up the whole potato plant to get potatoes, he discovered. All you have to do is wriggle your hand down into the dirt under the plant and feel around until you find some. It was as easy as putting your hand under a hen and getting eggs.

Planning ahead like this was already a habit for both of them. They had learned the hard way that when you're youngest in a greedy family, you always need to have a hidden supply.

They stopped at their stashing spot on the edge of the grove and left some of the oats and potatoes there.

When they came down the old people's driveway, they saw the old woman in the garden, cradling a big pan on her arm and picking strawberries. The old man hobbled along near the house carrying a long stick. The geese waddled around him. He was tending the geese. And their old black Chevy was back! It looked like a happy day all the way around.

"Well, well," said the old man. He had made his way to the middle of the yard with the geese. "Yeah, just go over there for a while," he said to them. He looked like an old dog herding sheep. "I'm keeping them away from the garden," he said to Henry and Gretchen. "Yep."

"We figured," said Henry.

They put their bikes down and showed what they'd brought. The old couple were happy to see the supplies. No "thank yous," just smiles.

"Sixer's comin along real nice," said the old man. "See her dancing and prancing around the yard all the time."

He didn't say anything about the extra legs. That was their first warning that maybe nothing had happened. And nothing had. Sixer trotted through the straw toward them with the extra legs wagging. Legs but no ponytail ties.

"It didn't work, it didn't work," said Gretchen. "Oh no."

"Nuts!" said Henry. They stood looking at Sixer. Nothing had changed. All that trouble for nothing!

"Let's see what those ties did," said Henry. "Let's see if maybe they're loose."

They knelt down and had a closer look. There wasn't even a mark where the ties had been. Henry held one extra leg and Gretchen the other. Sixer must have gotten rid of the ties before they'd gotten off the yard on their last visit. Not even a little crease in the wool.

"And I got my butt whupped for takin them ties," said Gretchen. "It's not fair."

They sat on their knees, each holding a leg. Sixer nuzzled them.

"She still knows us," said Gretchen. "Oh, sweety," she said, and rubbed the lamb's forehead.

"She ain't gettin sick or nothin," said Henry. "It sure don't look like she's gonna die."

"Don't die, Sixer," said Gretchen. "We're gonna get you fixed, just wait. We'll figure somethin out."

Together they rubbed and patted their lamb. The orange rectangle of a pupil seemed to look everywhere and nowhere, but her sniffing nose and wagging tail showed how happy she was to see them.

"If you don't look at them legs, she's perfect," said Gretchen. "Lookit this." She held her hands over the tops of Sixer's legs and leaned back to see what the lamb would look like without them.

"Perfect," said Gretchen.

"I know it," said Henry. "We'll figure somethin out." He rubbed his thumb along the top of one of the legs. "Maybe a knife. Not sure anymore. They do look like they're growin and probably got blood in 'em."

"Oouw," Gretchen moaned. "I don't want to cut Sixer."

"I don't neither," said Henry.

They kept rubbing the extra legs. The legs were cool on their hands, but not as cold as stone. They seemed half alive, like corn that's been nipped by frost but not quite killed off. Sixer put her nose to Gretchen's face, then to Henry's. At least that nose was alive! It wasn't hard to tell how the lamb felt about them. She was getting used to them and to the way they couldn't keep their hands off her extra legs.

Gretchen could smell the lamb's wool fat. She thought she could smell Henry too. His hair. She leaned a little bit toward him to see if she was right. It was his hair. It smelled like some kind of soap, but like straw too. He smelled sweet. Sort of. For the first time she noticed the fine hair on his tan arm, and the little dimple on his earlobe. Then she wondered about herself. What clothes had she put on this morning? Did she have on her old white socks or the clean blue ones? She tried to remember without looking at herself.

"Think she knows how terrible them legs look?" said Henry.

"Not probably," she said. "She ain't got nothin to compare."

Something moved in the straw along the sill of the old barn. A large rat looked out and sniffed in their direction. It twitched its wiry whiskers to make a piece of straw move away from its nose. Henry reached through the straw, picked up a clod, and threw it at the rat. The clod splattered against the barn wall and the rat *wssssed* out of sight.

"Maybe a rat will eat these things off," said Henry.

"Rats ate the toes off a baby at these one people's house once," said Gretchen.

"I'll bet," said Henry.

She looked at him, surprised. "It's true," she said.

"All right," he said.

They went back to petting Sixer and rubbing her extras. Henry watched Gretchen's hands. She had on pink fingernail polish, and he could hardly see the dirt under her fingernails. Her arm was skinnier than his. He already knew her legs were longer, and probably faster. He could see that even the back side of her calf was tan. If he had legs like that, he'd wear shorts too. He thought he could smell Gretchen, but he didn't lean toward her. He looked at her face from the side as she was petting the lamb. She was prettier than her sister even. She looked back at him for a second, and then they both looked down at Sixer and kept petting her.

With Sixer well-petted and well-fed, they went outside. The old man was herding the geese into the house.

"Come and eat, my little dumplings," said the old woman.

The old man had the geese trained, and he was shooing the last one up the stairs when Henry and Gretchen came in to sit down.

"You like brown sugar?" said the old woman. You could tell when she had the teeth by how clearly she talked.

Seeing the brown sugar, Henry remembered last winter. Brown sugar was the one thing he hadn't wanted

Granny to give away to the old couple. Brown sugar was kid food, not old-people food. Granny had said it was for cooking. Then he saw the bag—it was that same bag as last winter. So she hadn't used it for cooking. That's how wrong Granny had been about that brown sugar. By this time it had to be hard as a salt lick. But the old woman had put a slice of white bread in the bag of brown sugar to keep it soft. She pulled the bread out and it was as hard as a rusk, but he could see that the brown sugar was soft.

"Brown-sugar sandwiches," she said. "You kids like that?"

"Is it like syrup and bananas?" asked Gretchen. "Sounds pretty good. Never had one before."

"Sure," said Henry. He had.

The old woman smeared butter over the fresh bread, then spooned thick layers of brown sugar over it. Henry watched her old hands as she worked. She laid another slice of bread on the sugar and cut the sandwiches in two. Big spots on her hands were the same color as the brown sugar. Her knuckles were big and her fingernails were broken and dirty, but her hands worked a lot faster than Granny's. The soft butter started soaking up the brown sugar and turning the color of a cinnamon roll. She served them on the same plates she used for the pie. Maybe I can sneak her some new plates, thought Gretchen.

Everyone started digging their way to sugar heaven, the old woman chomping fast so she could get the teeth to the old man in a hurry. They were finished in no time, and the old man got up to go sit by the kitchen window. A goose honked from upstairs. Then a pig squealed from the hog yard, and the old man leaned forward to look out in the direction the sound. Maybe the animals had sensed that everyone was eating and wanted part of the action.

"They were ruining the garden," said the old woman.

"The pigs were?" said Gretchen.

"Them geese," said the old woman.

"We gotta keep 'em away from the foxes," said the old man.

"The pigs?" said Henry.

"Them geese," said the old man.

The pig squealed again, a loud, quick squeal that sounded like another pig had just given it a good bite on the ear.

"Gotta keep 'em out of the heat," said the old woman.

"The geese?" said Gretchen.

"Them pigs," said the old man. "Always fighting around the water trough. Yah."

"Come fall, we may have to butcher some of them critters," said the old woman.

"The pigs?" said Henry.

"Those pigeons under the eaves," said the old woman. "Don't you hear 'em? *Crghoo crghoo crghoo,*" she said. "I tell you."

"Yep. My, my," said the old man, and with the heel of his hand he tucked the teeth in tight.

"It sure is something," said the old woman.

"Uhm-boy," said the old man. "Yep."

Everybody sat quietly, looking at nothing in particular. The old man started rocking in his chair, overalls bunched up on his lap. The old woman put one elbow on the table and slowly rubbed her chin. Gretchen stared dreamily at her. She saw little red flowers growing on the old woman's dress. The flowers seemed to move, the way little flowers move on a warm summer day. The longer she looked at the dress, the brighter the flowers became, like a light was being turned up on them, like sunshine was coming from behind a cloud and making them redder. The redder they got, the bigger they got. She could see the little yellow dot in the middle of each flower and the little green stems that they were growing out of. Just sitting here like this, thought Gretchen . . . Life could be like this. No hassles.

Henry was relaxing too. It would have been so easy to put his head down on the table and take a little nap. But then a brown-sugar balloon blew itself up in his stomach and burped out and scared him.

"What was that?" said Gretchen, who seemed startled too.

"What time is it?" said Henry. "I bet it's getting late."

"You're right," said Gretchen. "We better be goin."

They slid their chairs out from the table and stood up.

As they were leaving, the old woman said, "Wait a minute." She put her hand on Gretchen's arm. "With the cinnamon you brought, maybe next time we could have some cinnamon rolls. But do you think you could find some more butter? We're almost out."

"No problem," said Henry.

"Piece of cake," said Gretchen.

"No, cinnamon rolls," said the old woman.

"They are pretty weird," said Henry as they biked along toward home. "And I'm feelin awful funny. I'm kinda dizzy and I almost fell asleep at the table."

Gretchen pedaled a little farther, looking at the smooth, worn tire track ahead of her. "That's odd," she said. "I'm feelin kinda yucky too. Dizzy. Kind of a funny headache. You don't think she's puttin stuff in the food, do ya?"

"They was eatin the same stuff we was," said Henry. "They wasn't gettin dizzy."

"You sure they was eatin the same stuff?"

Henry thought for a minute. "Come to think of it," he said, "maybe not. Their bread looked different."

They reached the intersection. "Listen," said Gretchen, "let's not split up yet, just in case we're gettin sick. We better stick together for a while. Let's go to my place, and if we're feelin all right we can go up in my treehouse and wait to see if we're gonna be all right."

"I don't want to croak up in your treehouse," said Henry. "If we're gonna get sick, let's get sick right here on the road where somebody will find us and get us to a doctor."

They rode around in the intersection for a few minutes. "This is crazy," said Gretchen. "I'm feelin fine. Let's just go to my treehouse and think about how we're gonna get Sixer's extras off."

They pedaled toward Gretchen's place, faster and faster as they got closer. "See," said Gretchen, "we're feelin fine."

"I think so," said Henry.

Panting, they parked their bikes, then made their way through the grove to her treehouse. Henry climbed up without any help from Gretchen this time. He sat down on his cushion and looked out through the opening between the branches.

Gretchen sat down beside him. "We're not sick," she said. "We need to worry about Sixer's legs, not our stomachs and heads." She pulled her knees to her chin and wrapped her arms around them. "I like to come up here," she said. "It helps me think straight. I have good ideas up here."

"Makes sense," said Henry. "The higher up you are, the closer you are to God maybe."

"You think so?" said Gretchen.

"Makes sense, don't it?" he said.

They sat for a while on their grass mats, staring out through the opening, just staring out toward the clouds and sky. A nice breeze was blowing and only once did Henry have to swat at a mosquito before Gretchen said, "I got it! I got a idea! Wart-remover stuff! My creepy sister had this big wart on her knuckle, see, and Mom got this wart-remover stuff and it come right off. Wish it had been her nose."

"That'll never work," said Henry. "Sixer's legs ain't warts."

"Same idea," she said. "You got somethin growin where it ain't supposed to be. Same idea."

"Wart remover," said Henry. "I'd like to put some all over my brothers' heads."

"We could smear gobs of it all around the top of both of the extras," said Gretchen.

They sat quietly and stared into the clouds that were moving slowly across the sky in big puffy clumps.

"Maybe instead we should pray that those extras fall off," said Henry.

"Moses went to a mountaintop to pray," said Gretchen. "This is like a mountaintop."

"He wasn't prayin for nobody's legs to fall off, was he?" said Henry.

"I forget what he was prayin about," said Gretchen, "but maybe we shouldn't try prayin 'em off. My mom says we mustn't pray that the wicked perish. We oughta pray that the wicked see the light."

"So?" said Henry. "What's Sixer's extras got to do with the wicked perishin?"

"You gotta be careful about prayin is what I'm sayin," said Gretchen. "I prayed once that I'd get a pony for my birthday. We was so poor there was no way anybody could buy me a pony. So that time prayin didn't work. But then one time I prayed the ice on the roads would melt so I could go visit my cousin. That worked."

"You prayed the ice off'n the roads?" said Henry.

"Sorta," she said. "I prayed in the morning and *psst,* just like that, the sun burned all that ice away and I got to go play at my cousin's house and we had loads of fun. You shouldn't oughta pray for things you want. You gotta pray for things you don't want. For things you want to go away. Like that ice. Like Sixer's extras maybe. That's how prayin works best."

"Not sure," said Henry. "We're not supposed to be goin over to the old couple's house and we ain't told nobody about Sixer. Maybe it would be bad luck to pray for somethin when we're someplace we're not supposed to be. Maybe it would be like prayin that you didn't get caught snitchin cookies."

Gretchen thought about that one. "Maybe we ain't supposed to be at the old people's house," she said, "but tryin to pray Sixer's extras off ain't like snitchin cookies. Maybe it's a sin to be at the old couple's place, but that don't mean everything we do there is more sin. Sin ain't about where you are."

"It ain't?" said Henry.

"Sin is about what you do," she said.

"You sure?"

"Yep," she said.

They sat and thought some more. "This is like one of them story problems in arithmetic," said Henry. "They mix you up."

"Prayin won't hurt," said Gretchen. "Not the way a knife might."

"Knife ain't always bad," said Henry. "They cut the tails off some dogs, you know. They saw the horns off bulls so they don't go stickin ya through the guts. I seen this one farmer, he cut the tips off all the beaks on his chickens so they couldn't peck each other. Cuttin can be good."

"Guess so," said Gretchen. "Mom says if you cut the little thing under a crow's tongue, that crow can talk. And they cuts the ears on some dogs so the ears stick straight up. And there's casseratin," she added.

"Yep," he said.

"So we gonna try prayin or not?" she said.

"Okay," he said. "We'll try prayin about it. But let's don't pray out loud. That might be bad luck. Let's pray quiet in our heads. Just in case it ain't all right."

"We're not even at the old couple's house right now," she said. "I'm gonna pray out loud."

"I'm not," said Henry.

Gretchen got right into it. "Dear Almighty Father in heaven," she said.

"Shh," said Henry.

"If it be Thine almighty will, Almighty Father, take off them funny legs from Thy servant Sixer. And keep them off. For Jesus' sake, Amen."

Henry kept his hands folded as he prayed quietly to himself. Gretchen watched him. It was a long prayer. Henry was praying so hard that he sounded like he was snoring. He went on and on and his breathing got louder and louder. He swayed a little, and Gretchen put her hand on his arm to keep him from tipping over.

"Break your neck prayin, that would take the cake," she said softly.

"Almost done," he said softly back to her.

He opened his eyes. Her hand was still on his arm.

It was a lot warmer than Sixer's extras. "Your arm got warmer and warmer as you was prayin," she said. "Maybe your prayer was workin. Fire of the Holy Spirit."

Gretchen folded her hands to pray again. She closed her eyes. This time she whispered, "Oh merciful Jesus at the right hand of God, at the throne of the Father Almighty in Heaven . . ."

Before she could finish, Henry started saying his prayer out loud too. "Let them fall to the earth," he said. "Let Sixer be in perfect shape."

"Dear God," said Gretchen, "that it be Thy will, let Sixer be a perfect little lamb."

"Amen," they said together.

They looked up at the sky and stared into the clouds some more. A big white lamb formed in one of them. It floated along in the air without moving its legs, cruising along as if there was nothing to it. One eye of the lamb was hidden, but the other one looked straight at Henry and Gretchen, almost as if it were asking them a question. Then they saw the extras hanging on the front of this lamb. The lamb slowly turned toward them, its hindquarters moving in the sky while its head stayed in one place. It was Sixer, and she was turning in the sky to look straight down on them. Now both of the cloudy sheep's eyes were trained right on Henry and Gretchen, where they sat on their grass cushions. One of the extras started to move away from the lamb's chest and fizzle away like the bubbles on a glass of soda pop.

"Did you see that?" said Gretchen.

" 'Course I saw that," said Henry.

"That's Sixer up there. God is showing us somethin."

"I know it," said Henry.

A crow cawed, close by. "That's it," said Henry. "That was a sign from heaven."

Gretchen's face brightened with a wide smile and wide eyes. She looked out through the opening in the trees into the promising sky.

"You're right!" she said. "That crow cawin there. That was it. Sixer's legs must've fell off right then when that crow cawed. Hallelujah!"

"Don't say that," said Henry. "We gotta be careful not to be too happy. It would be bad luck, I just know it. That cawing probably just meant God heard us and He's probably thinkin about it."

"What do you mean?" said Gretchen. "God sent us Sixer in the sky to show exactly how He was gonna do it." She wriggled her fingers in a sprinkling motion to remind him how the extras on Sixer in the clouds had dissolved into thin air. "Let's go look. Come on!"

"No no no," said Henry. "We mustn't get pushy with God. We gotta wait for a little bit. We'll go look tomorrow."

"All right," she said.

"I don't feel sick at all anymore, do you?" said Henry.

" 'Course not," she said. "There's healin in the air."

THIRTEEN

———————

Grace and Wart Remover

WHEN THEY WERE PRAYING in Gretchen's treehouse, it was as if for a little while they weren't the youngest. Nobody was there to tell them that their ideas weren't important because they were the least important people in their families. But praying had meant that for a little while their thoughts could soar straight up into heaven, and heaven itself could come down to them in the form of Sixer in the clouds showing how God would let her extras dissolve. God had even used the crow to tell them how much He had heard them. "The same way God sent a owl to show me where the treehouse was," Gretchen had said.

Overnight the weather had shifted and brought a few showers that gave the corn a good shot in the arm and settled the dust on the gravel roads. The morning air was fresh and cool, filled with the sweet smells of clover and blooming roadside flowers as Henry and Gretchen biked toward the old couple's place.

For a few minutes the only sound was the crickets in the ditch grass and the *hum-swish* sounds of their bike tires. Henry wore clean jeans and a clean green T-shirt with a little pocket on the chest. Gretchen wore a clean blue shirt and jeans and had tied a red kerchief over her ponytail tie. She looked over to Henry and said, "You think animals can pray?"

"I think they can wish things," said Henry.

"I was just gettin worried," said Gretchen. "I was worried that maybe we're not supposed to ask God's grace on animals."

"You prayed ice off the roads once," said Henry. "Why you worryin about prayin Sixer's extras off?"

"I don't want to be messin with God's grace," she said.

"I never got that 'grace' stuff," said Henry. "That's church talk. How's it different from good luck and bad luck?"

"Grace is what God gives people. Maybe animals. Bad luck is what you brung on yourself."

"Bad luck is what the old couple got. They ain't as rich as some folks and maybe not quite as smart neither. They didn't do nothin to get that bad luck."

"You don't know that. Maybe they did give themselves their bad luck," said Gretchen. "Maybe we should pray for them next time."

Henry imagined an extra set of false teeth appearing in the clouds so the old couple could each have their own. That would be some grace, he thought, but he didn't laugh. "I think it's like when you're lucky," said Henry. "That's grace. Like if somebody shoots at you and misses. That's grace. But it's people mostly gets the grace. Animals ain't usually so lucky."

"I knew this lucky mouse once," said Gretchen. "That little sucker must've had hisself some grace for sure. That little pepper would set off one mousetrap after another and never get squished. *Blap blap blap*, all those mousetraps would snap shut, but never got this one mouse."

"Maybe he was just smart," said Henry. "Maybe he stuck a stick or somethin in them traps."

"Nosiree," said Gretchen. "That little mouse was real lucky or somethin. Nothin could get that mouse. And he'd go and eat the cheese after he set those mousetraps off."

"That sounds like grace to me," said Henry.

"But can you pray grace on somethin? That's what I'm wonderin," said Gretchen. "Could we pray grace on Sixer? Grace them friggin legs off?"

"God could take those legs off a hunnert times just while we're pedalin along here," said Henry. "If he likes what we're sayin, maybe he keeps 'em off. If he don't, he probably just sticks 'em right back on. Shucks, taking stupid extra legs on and off a lamb is as easy for God as screwing a cap on and off a catsup bottle."

"So let's put God in a good mood before we get there," said Gretchen. "Let's sing."

"All right, you start," he said.

" 'What a feee-rend we have in Jeeeee-zus,' " she sang.

"Not that one!" he yelled.

"All right then, you start!" she yelled.

" 'You are my sun-shine, my only sun-shine . . .' "

She was with him on this one. They sang and made their way down the driveway of the old couple's place. Just how exactly did God do it? Did the extras fizzle off the way they did in the cloud? Would Sixer feel the extras leaving her body, and if she did, would she know that it was God's grace working on her, or would she think it was just one of those things, like hail falling from the sky or the wind blowing against her wool?

There was no sign of the old couple or the geese as they pulled up beside the barn. They could hear Sixer running through the straw. She was celebrating all right.

When they swung open the door, Sixer came dancing toward them—and she had changed. But not for the better. The extras were still dangling under her chin, but they were covered with manure. She had been sleeping in the manure pile.

"Oh no," said Gretchen. "No! No! No!" She held her hands to her face. She was almost crying.

Henry pinched his lips together and stared at the manure-packed extras. "I knew we shouldn't've been talkin about this so much," he said. "I knew that would be bad luck."

"We should've finished 'What a Friend We Have in Jesus,' " said Gretchen. "That's what we should've done. You and your stupid singin ideas."

"Not my fault," said Henry. "And I don't know 'What a Friend We Have in Jesus' all the way to the end. Don't go blamin me."

"Not my fault neither, so don't go blamin me neither!" She stamped her foot in the straw and clenched her fists.

Sixer would have none of their arguing. She bucked and danced and would have been singing if she knew how. She jumped and spun around and teased them to try catching her. She broke right through their bad feelings and got them to join in with her, chasing and grabbing until they caught her. Then she nuzzled them and stood still, waiting for their hands to rub her forehead and nose.

"We can't be fightin," said Gretchen. "We gotta clean her up."

"Who's fightin?" said Henry.

"Come on, get some straw," said Gretchen.

Henry and Gretchen knelt down and rubbed Sixer's extras clean from the grime she'd gotten caked on them.

"I wonder where we could put the wart-remover stuff," said Henry.

"You'd put wart remover on 'em after we prayed to get 'em off?" said Gretchen. "What you think God would think of that? That would hurt God's feelings, that's what it would do, and that would make Him mad. Fat chance anybody'd have for grace if we start slingin wart remover on the very thing we prayed about."

"So what?" said Henry. "God didn't take the extras

off. And He fooled us to boot, sending Sixer in a cloud, and then that silly crow."

"The crow didn't say God had done it for sure," said Gretchen. "It was just a sign. Maybe we should've held the extras while we was prayin. Ain't that 'layin on of hands'?"

"You do the layin on of hands," said Henry, "and I'll sprinkle on the wart remover. Give 'em a double blast."

"You're makin fun," said Gretchen. "God hears that."

"He wasn't listenin last time," said Henry.

"Stop talkin like that," she said. "Talk about bad luck, that's bad luck. My mom says you make fun of things and those things'll happen to you. Like you must never make fun of a cripple."

She stood up and crossed her hands. She looked serious about this.

"There was this one kid in North Dakota," she said, "and he walked behind this old cripple man making fun of the way this old cripple man was walkin, and a car come and run right over this kid's leg that he was makin fun with. Talk about a cripple, that kid's a cripple."

"You know him?"

"No, but I seen him," said Gretchen. "In this one town in North Dakota. He walks like a duck now, and now all the other kids make fun of him."

"All them other kids makin fun of him, there's gonna be an awful lot of people walkin like ducks in that town," said Henry.

"You're makin fun of me," said Gretchen. "And I don't like it!"

"All right, all right," he said. "Don't be so touchy."

"You're the touchy one," she said. "Get grumpy every time somethin don't go the way you want it."

Sixer moved in again before Henry could answer Gretchen. Sixer rubbed against Henry's leg, wagging her tail. She was as happy as ever, even happier it seemed. Henry and Gretchen quit arguing and rubbed Sixer's ears and forehead while the extra legs hung there, cleaner now but untouched by luck or grace.

"Time to eat!" they heard the old woman yelling. "Come on, you little snapper-whippers."

As soon as they were out of the barn, they could smell the aroma of fresh cinnamon rolls coming through the kitchen window.

"See you've been taking good care of Sixer," said the old man as they settled down at their usual places around the table. "These are the best kids I ever seen," he said to the old woman. "Look, even the cocklebur is almost smiling."

Henry tried not to smile. He moved his big eyebrows down over his eyes and looked up at the old man.

"And this little flax princess," said the old woman. "Put some flesh on her cheeks and she'll have a smiley face."

"So how come I'm seeing frowns around this table today?" said the old man.

"We was hopin the legs would come off," said Gretchen.

Henry looked at her sharply. He had thought the

praying was a matter just between the two of them. Now he was gearing up for some embarrassing talk. Gretchen was sitting up straight as if she was gearing up for some straight talk.

"We've tried everything to get them off except cuttin," she said.

"I getcha," said the old man. "I seen your rubber bands. That was a pretty clever idea. Yah."

"We tried prayin," said Gretchen. Henry looked down at his plate.

"Yah, that won't hurt either," said the old man.

The old woman was busy cutting up cinnamon rolls at the counter, but she was listening.

"We just do our best, don't we?" said the old woman.

"Yah," said the old man. "Do your best and take what comes. Yah."

"Maybe we should just leave them alone," said Gretchen. "She is pretty healthy the way she looks. I dunno." She watched as the old woman shoveled a big square cinnamon roll onto a plate in front of her. Sticky brown-sugar sauce dripped down the side. "I did know a girl with six toes once," said Gretchen. "In North Dakota. She's doin all right I guess."

"A girl with six toes?" said Henry. "I'll bet."

"It's true," said Gretchen.

"A little extra, a little less, people get along the same way," said the old woman.

"Yep," said the old man. "Half full or half empty, same thing."

"Six of one and half dozen of the other," said the old woman.

"Yep," said the old man.

"You knew a girl with six toes?" said Henry. "So was she like that cripple kid from North Dakota you was talkin about?"

"No," said Gretchen. "She wasn't cripple or nothin. She just had one shoe that was bigger than the other one."

The old man put a hand on his bad hip and twisted himself in his chair.

"That musta been funny, seein this one big foot and this one little one!" said Henry.

"No funnier than Sixer," said Gretchen.

"You eat now, my little raspberry," said the old woman.

"But did she like trip over that big shoe and everything?" said Henry.

"You get used to what you don't have," said the old woman.

"Yep," said the old man. "Enough is plenty when you have enough. Yah. Us cripples get along."

Gretchen was the first to realize that talking about bad toes and cripples was not the nicest thing to do around the old man. She looked at him. He didn't look mad, but he was staring at her. Gretchen gave Henry a good nudge.

"Did you laugh at her?" said Henry.

Gretchen gave him another good nudge. "You don't laugh at cripples," she said.

"Good to see some grub on the table," the old man said, and pulled up his sleeves as he leaned over to sniff the cinnamon roll. Gretchen noticed that his fist was rolled tight. She gave Henry another good nudge. He got it. He looked at the old man. He saw the rolled fist too.

"Geese could eat the grubs," said the old lady.

"Geese eat grubs off'n the table?" said Gretchen. She checked around her plate. Maybe dirty food and bugs is what made them feel sick last time.

"No no," said the old man. "Geese eat grubs off the ground."

"Only thing they eat off the ground is strawberries," said the old lady.

"Yah. Well," said the old man, "when they're in the garden, at least they put some manure on the strawberries."

"I'd rather put cream and sugar on my strawberries," said the old woman.

"Well, geese are upstairs now," said the old man. "That's one way to keep them off the ground."

"Isn't this the ground floor?" said Gretchen.

"Oh, no," said the old woman. "This is the wooden floor. Now stop asking so many questions, my little sunbeam, and eat your grub."

When the old woman handed the old man the teeth, Henry looked at his own hands. They smelled a little bit like Sixer's extras before they cleaned them off. It was too late to stop now. "I better use a fork," he said.

Gretchen sniffed her hands. "Me too," she said.

After their little feast, the old man said to Henry and Gretchen, "Why don't you two go upstairs and see the geese before you go home. I think they'd like to see you."

"Oh, that would be a good idea," said the old woman. "The children have been waiting for you, and maybe they'd like some cinnamon rolls too."

"Not this time," said Gretchen. "I gotta go get eggs."

She slid her chair back and started around the table. She watched the old man as she headed toward the door. He didn't get up to try to stop her. Henry saw how quickly Gretchen was moving and followed close behind her.

"What's wrong?" said Henry as they biked away.

"I just ain't sure no more," said Gretchen. "There's somethin real scary about the old man. I used to think the old woman was the weird one, but she just talks weird. You see the way he rolled up his fist when we was talkin about that girl with six toes? He thought we was makin fun of him. Maybe the way the kid on the Fourth of July made fun of him."

"You was the one talkin," said Henry. "You gettin scared of them?"

"It just makes you wonder," said Gretchen, "if there's anyplace that's safe, you know. I mean I go home and I catch it there. Now you're my friend and you start blamin me for stuff. We got Sixer but she's got these stupid legs. Then the old man rolls up his fist and it makes me think of that boy who got his leg broke by the old man's bumper, makes me wonder if we're next, you know."

"You think that boy the old man hit is a cripple now? Like that kid in North Dakota who walks like a duck? Or maybe like that girl with six toes you was talkin about?"

"Stop it!" yelled Gretchen. "You're makin fun. You're always makin fun when I'm tryin to be serious."

Gretchen sped up and Henry had to pump as hard as he could to catch up with her. "Hey," he said. "We're friends, remember? Things ain't so bad. Let's sing the rest of the way to the intersection and be friends again."

She pedaled in silence until they got closer to the intersection. "All right," she said. "I'll start. 'You are my sun-shine, my only sun-shine . . .' "

Henry joined in and they sang it three times before they parted ways at the intersection.

What they didn't know is that what waited for them at home was anything but sunshine. Gretchen's folks knew she'd been going over to the old couple's house. So did Henry's. Granny and Gretchen's mother had been talking about it on the telephone. Henry and Gretchen's secret was no longer a secret—at least not all of it.

FOURTEEN

The Secret Is Out

IT WOULD HAVE BEEN ONE THING if Henry's father had been the first one to talk to him about going to the old couple's place, but no, of course it had to be his mean brothers who brought it up. They were the thunder before the storm.

"And Dad knows you're goin over there with that skinny girl with glasses from North Dakota. Dad's gonna take your bike away if you don't stop it." That was big Jake, who must have thought that being biggest meant he could always be the one to break bad news.

"We just go for rides," said Henry.

"You're ridin on thin ice with Dad," said smart-alecky Josh.

What did they think he was going to do all day if he

wasn't going off with Gretchen? Henry wondered. Wreck the play farm? Tease their dumb 4-H calves?

But Henry knew his father was the only real "Says who?" in their house, and it was his dad who had his say on the matter.

"Having a pretty good summer then?" his father asked as they walked across the yard. His father breathed loud through his nose. Always. It was embarrassing in church.

"Pretty good," said Henry.

"Been getting around quite a bit on your bike then?"

"Quite a bit," said Henry.

"That North Dakota girl likes to ride her bike pretty good too then?"

So he really did know. Henry could feel something bad coming. "She's got a red Schwinn," he said.

His father's breathing was getting louder and louder. "We've been talking to the North Dakota girl's folks," he said. "They were asking about the old couple, what you two do over there. They saw the old couple at The Grove on the Fourth. They heard the old man hit a little boy with his car and the police took the car away from him."

Henry wasn't ready to be put in this kind of a pickle. He had his own worries about the old man, but the last thing he needed was help in his worrying from his and Gretchen's dads. Henry thought fast: If the old man goes, there goes Sixer, there go the cinnamon rolls, and maybe even Gretchen.

"That wasn't his fault," Henry blurted out in a voice

that was a lot louder than he expected. "Everybody was teasin the old couple, and this little kid thought he could do it too. That's what happened."

"Hold on, hold on," said his father. "We know they finally decided it was an accident and he got his car back. Not everybody thought it was an accident, though. It looked like the old man stepped on the gas right when that little boy got there. They dropped the charges against the old man, but he's not allowed to drive some places anymore, just to the grocery store."

"Can't go blamin the old man," said Henry. "Why don't they blame them boys who stuck a firecracker on that gopher and blew it to smitereens?"

"Hold on, hold on," said his father. "Let's not just talk about what happened on the Fourth of July. What do you two do when you go over to the old couple's place?"

"Nothin," said Henry.

"Nothing? You don't have to bike all the way over there to do nothing."

"We help them a little bit with chores," he said. "The old folks have it kind of hard to get around anymore. So me and the North Dakota girl, we feed oats to the lamb over there."

"Lamb?" said his father. "Since when did the old man start raising sheep? I never heard that. You need to know what you're doing to make money with sheep. They can't afford to lose any money. They're living off the county and the neighbors the way it is."

"Just one sheep," said Henry. "And he got that one free at the sale barn."

"Free? What's wrong with it?" said his father.

"The North Dakota girl and me, we take care of it, that's all."

"What do you know about sheep?" said his father.

"The North Dakota girl, she knows about sheep," said Henry. "They had sheep in North Dakota."

"Her dad says sheep almost drove them into the ground," said his father. "And what's wrong with this sheep?"

"It's a lamb," said Henry.

His father studied him, as if he was trying to size up this whole situation. Why did he have to think something was fishy? Why couldn't he just settle for a little bit of the truth? If he told his father that the lamb was named Sixer, his father would want to know why such a funny name, and then his brothers would find out and the teasing would never stop. It was bad enough that they were making fun of Gretchen's glasses. He could about imagine what they'd say if they knew about their pet Sixer being a freak that the crazy old man had given them. And if he told the truth about Sixer, how long would it be before his father knew that he was eating at the house of people who had only one pair of false teeth between the two of them? There had to be a better way. To tell his father any more would be like pulling one ear of corn from the pile. Pretty soon the whole corncrib full of corn comes rolling down on top of you and you get swallowed up by all that truth-telling.

"The old couple have you coming over there to feed a lamb, that what you're saying?"

"The old couple don't have us come over there for

nothin. We just like this lamb and they let us pet it. What's wrong with that anyhow?"

"Are you going in the house there?"

"Maybe to get a drink of water," said Henry. "How come everybody gots it in for the old couple anyways?"

"You can't trust them, that's why," said his father. "There's bad blood there."

His father led Henry into the hog house and sat down on a bale of straw. "Let me tell you a few things," he said.

Here it came. Henry had heard the story of the old couple before, but this time his father gave him both barrels. When he was a teenager, the old man had accidentally shoved a friend into the threshing machine when they were pitching bundles into the machine. They were fooling around, pushing each other on the wagon-load of bundles. Henry already knew that story, but it was an accident, after all. After the accident, though, no one would have anything to do with the old man. Certainly no decent girl. So he had married this wild girl from the next county who had no religion at all. The farm they lived on had belonged to the old man's father, but the old couple had lost almost all the land during the Depression. All they had left was five acres with the buildings and grove. Most people thought they had got what they had coming to them, and nobody was surprised that their one son was a troublemaker too, and that he had ended up in a mental hospital.

"They just have bad luck," said Henry.

"Bad luck can be catchy," said his father. "We don't

want them starving to death, but we don't want them passing on their ways to you kids either. The North Dakota girl's folks feel the same way."

"But we gotta go over there and take care of the lamb," said Henry. "We promised."

"All right, but you're going to make another promise today," said his father. "You're going to promise to do nothing over there except feed this lamb. That should be all right."

"All right," said Henry.

"One other thing," said his father. "I want you to go to your room and pray about this. You go and pray that there will never be any false words on your tongue. And you pray that the Lord will protect you against any false words the old couple might say to you. Understand?"

"Understand," said Henry.

That afternoon Granny was going to town for groceries. His older brothers were going with his father to pick cockleburs from the corn on the back forty. And Henry had to stay home. No bicycle riding, no playing in the grove. He was supposed to go to his room and pray the afternoon away. Pray that he wouldn't lie? That and pray that God would protect him from the evils of the old couple. What would God think of this kind of praying anyhow? Henry had never heard the like.

But alone he was in the stuffy mid-afternoon air of the house. He had been *left* alone. Granny and his dad didn't understand the difference between that and when it was his own idea to go off and be alone, which he did so that he'd be free to be himself instead of that somebody everybody else wanted him to be. But when he was *left* alone, he got that empty feeling. Maybe this was the way it would be someday. Since he was youngest, maybe someday they'd all be gone and he'd be the only one left. In the end, he'd be the one who got left behind.

Stay in the house and *pray* all afternoon? He certainly had enough time to do more than that. Praying to try to get Sixer's extras off had only taken about five minutes, and that had practically worn him out.

After Granny had been gone for over fifteen minutes and when Henry could hear that the tractor was nearly a half mile away from the house, he decided to go into the basement and have a look at Granny's living quarters. She never invited him down there. It was an even bigger mess than he expected it would be, with knitting stuff and unfolded clothes all over the place. The only thing that had a neat place was Granny's old camera, which sat in a little black box on her chest of drawers. He checked her little refrigerator. It was exactly as he always suspected. It was stuffed full of sweet stuff. A couple dozen cookies in the bottom part, and in the freezer compartment three quarts of ice cream! Strawberry, chocolate, and his favorite—butter brickle. That was the same kind his mother had always got them as a special treat. Butter brickle. Once you've had butter brickle, you never forget it. And these chocolate-chip cookies—they were exactly the kind his mother had always made. Why couldn't Granny share these if she was going to steal ideas from his mother? So much food in here. So this is where all the grocery money was going. The butter brickle was the only container open, so he took a couple of spoonfuls of it. Then he took two chocolate-chip cookies and rearranged the rest so nobody would be able to tell that any were missing. He went back upstairs with mixed-up feelings, not because he had taken a little food that Granny would be better off without, but because Granny's living place was such a sad sight. It was hard to feel sorry for anybody who couldn't keep their space neater than that. Even the old woman had a neater kitchen than Granny's room. She hadn't even made her bed.

When Henry was back upstairs, he noticed how much time he still had and decided to go check out his father's bedroom. On his way to the bedroom, he stopped in the front room to play piano. He tried his hand at a hymn his mother used to play, "Jesus, Lover of My Soul." It was an easy one, but his left hand wouldn't switch chords at the right time. He gave up on it and went into his father's bedroom.

This is the room where his father slept alone now, though Henry knew that lots of times his father slept on the front-room couch, pulled a blanket over himself and slept through the night after watching the ten o'clock news.

Henry didn't remember if it was a rule not to, but none of the boys ever went into this bedroom. They just didn't go in there. That was Dad and Mom's room. Henry almost changed his mind and turned back when he stepped in and closed the door behind him. It was the smell. The room still smelled like his mother after all these years. He wasn't sure what it was. Not perfume exactly, but a sweet, clean smell. Almost like a clean white towel with a rose wrapped so tight inside it that you could hardly smell the rose as much as the cleanness of the towel. It was her smell, not as strong as when she was alive, but it was still there. After more than five years. He was really little when she died, but this smell—it was like yesterday. He sniffed the curtain in front of the closet to find out if that was where his mother's smell was coming from. That wasn't it exactly. He checked the bedspread and pillows. It wasn't there. He looked under the bed. Nothing there but dust balls. If Granny was supposed to be taking care of things, why couldn't she at least dust under his father's bed once in a while, instead of just grumping around and watching soap operas all the time?

Henry walked around the bed sniffing, trying to figure out where his mother's smell was coming from. He sniffed the curtains. The wallpaper. He couldn't find it. The smell wasn't coming from anything in particular. The smell of his mother was coming from everywhere in this room.

Finally, he opened the bottom drawer of the dresser. Nobody had taken his mother's underskirts and stockings out of there. Henry put his nose into the drawer, but it didn't have the mother smell that he was sensing. He pulled open the next drawer. There weren't any clothes in this drawer. It was full of boxes with big brown-covered picture albums in them. These were the albums his dad was always messing with after supper or on Sunday afternoons. Henry pulled out the top one and walked over to the bed with it. He opened the big brown cover and started paging through the black pages. Page after page of old people in this one, some of them with horses and buggies, one with a bunch of people around a threshing machine, one with an old man with a beard and an old woman with a hat, both of them sitting on picnic chairs on somebody's lawn. Henry remembered them—they were his great-grandma and -grandpa who came from the Old Country and never learned to speak English. Their faces were wrinkled and stern. What sour faces. They looked like the most unhappy people on the face of the earth. He went back for another album.

This one had pictures of his mom and dad in it. They didn't look all that happy in their wedding picture. She looked afraid and he looked like somebody who had just pulled a fast one and was thinking twice about it now. Whose idea of a joke was his mom's hairdo anyways? It looked like a bundle of oats on top of her head. And her little eyes looked scared, like she knew all along that something terrible would happen before her kids were big. At least this was before she started putting on weight. He looked hard at her round face and wondered what his father saw in her. Then he looked at his father's hard face and wondered what his mother saw in him. Maybe the eyebrows. They really were something. He touched his own and was glad they weren't quite as big as his dad's. All the pictures in this album were of Dad and Mom before there were any kids. There was one nice one. It was out in the back of the field under the willow tree that was still there. It looked like she had just brought him a pail of lunch and they had been lying on a blanket out there. They were hugging each other and smiling. Who took that picture anyhow?

Henry went back for another album. This one had the kids in it. Three or four pages of his mom with his brothers, and then one, two, three, four, five, six pictures of himself—covering two pages. It was him in diapers playing with toys. The next page was more of him, all of these with his mother in the picture with him, sometimes holding him on her lap, sometimes playing with him on the front-room floor. Why didn't she ever play with his brothers like this? Maybe they couldn't afford the film before he was born.

On the next page were still more pictures of him and his mother. Henry didn't remember ever seeing any of these pictures before. She almost looked happy in one of these pictures, smiling and pointing. Maybe she didn't know she was in that picture. There was one with his mother on the floor, coloring pictures with him in a big coloring book. What ever happened to that coloring book anyhow?

Henry was sure the next page would be of something different—but it wasn't! It was still more pictures of him and his mother. Six more pictures of nothing but him and his mother! There he was at the piano, his chin about even with the keys and both hands up there plunking away. He must have been about two. And the rest of the pictures? They were all of him and his mother at the piano. One with him a little older on her lap and she's showing him where to put his fingers. And one when he was even older and he's sitting beside her playing on the low-note side. That had to be it—she was showing him how to play "Indian Dance."

He turned the page really expecting something after that. But there was nothing. And nothing again on the next page. Two black pages. On these pages his mother was dead.

Henry was sweating. He felt hungry, but he knew Granny hadn't left any goodies in the kitchen, and he figured he'd better not push his luck by digging around in her basement refrigerator again. He kicked his shoes off and lay back on the bed. He lay in the middle, his head in the crack between the two pillows. He could remember when his crib was still in this room, before he was old enough to sleep upstairs. He remembered crying so that his mother would pick him up and put him on this very spot between herself and his father.

He put his hands on his stomach and stared at the ceiling. He didn't feel like crying. He felt more like breaking one of his brothers' bikes or spitting in somebody's soup when they weren't looking. He pulled a button off his shirt and threw it at the window. It bounced back and under the bed. He felt more relaxed now and closed his eyes. He heard a pig squealing. It sounded trapped, like it had its head caught in something. But taking care of the pigs was his brothers' job, and he wasn't about to go out there and do their work when he was left behind.

He kept his eyes closed and saw Sixer standing against the darkness of his eyelids. The extras hung under her chin like two strands of wool that could easily be pulled off. He could feel something good starting to happen in the world, something peaceful moving across his chest and face. Was he praying?

When he woke up, his father was standing over him, his eyes as fiery as a monster's and his big bristly eyebrows looking like wire as sharp as claws. "Get out of this bed!" he said. "Out!"

FIFTEEN

Four Eyes and Horse Teeth

GRETCHEN FOUND OUT that her folks knew about her visits to the old couple's house when her mother dropped the butter dish on the floor as she was setting the table for noon dinner.

"That does it," she said. "If I'm not worried about one daughter, I'm worried about the other." She started to stamp her foot but changed her mind when she saw she was going to stamp on a piece of broken glass, and then almost tripped herself. "We know you and that boy from over yonder are going to that strange old couple's house," she said. "And we don't like it."

"We're not doin nothin wrong," said Gretchen. She glanced at Jo-Anne. Big Sis was probably the snitch.

Her father sat at his place at the table, rubbing his bald head and looking sad.

"Those old people don't even go to church," her mother said, "and you're going over there without an adult. What kind of ideas do you think can come from those kind of people? We moved away from North Dakota to get away from heathens." She jittered to the porch for a broom and dustpan. Back in the kitchen, she said, "Your father is going to have a good talk with you before you even think of going over there again."

"We just go and feed this pet sheep," said Gretchen.

"Sheep?" said her mother. "Did I hear you say *sheep*? As if this family hasn't had its fill of sheep!"

"It's just a little pet lamb," said Gretchen. "We just help take care of this pet lamb."

Everybody quieted down as Gretchen's mother cleaned up.

"You're not planning to bring that lamb home to this farm, are you, young lady?" said her father.

"Oh no," said Gretchen. "We just go over there and feed it. Oh boy, cream corn!" she said.

That worked. Everybody was looking at the food now. They all sat down and folded their hands for the opening prayer. "Our Father who knowest all things," Gretchen's father began, "we come unto Thee beseeching Thy mercy upon us, Thy unworthy children."

Gretchen opened her eyes. Maybe she could take some of God's mercy away from Jo-Anne if she kept her eyes open and stared at her.

"Stand with us in the hour of temptation," her father went on, "lest we fall to the fiery darts of the Evil One."

Gretchen closed her eyes.

"Be our rock and our foundation in the midst of

worldly travail," her father prayed in his earnest voice, "oh heavenly Father, even until the end of time or until the end of our earthly sojourn. Bless now this food unto our bodies. May it sustain us in our needs to do the work that Thou hast prepared for us to do on this earth. Oh Lord, may this fruit of our labors make us mindful of the great feast that awaits us at Thy right hand with Thy faithful Son our Lord and Shepherd Jesus Christ, in whose name we pray, Amen."

Gretchen and Jo-Anne quickly followed with, "Heavenly Father, be our guest. May this food to us be blessed, Amen."

They dug in, but bad feelings were floating through the air, thick as the stench of the hog yards. Jo-Anne had been out late last night at the teenage night-swim at the sandpit. She was sleep-eating now, about one bite a minute. She actually put one elbow on the table and plunked her chin down on her hand. Then with the other hand she shoveled in the food. You could almost hear her snore between bites. And what a sight with her hair sticking everywhere and her bathrobe still on and bunched around her neck.

Gretchen knew she would have to take the first step to brighten things up when a dark shadowy mood had settled down on them. All she did was say a few things about Jo-Anne's bathrobe. Like, "You sure don't cover that much of your skinny body when you're in your skimpy bathing suit. Why don't you wear your bathrobe to the night-swim so people don't have to look at your string-bean body, huh?"

That didn't seem to get anybody's attention. They

just went on chewing their food and staring down at their plates. Just as Jo-Anne was hoisting up a mouthful of creamed corn, Gretchen said, "You oughta seen her that time we was at the sandpit together. First she goes and wiggles her butt so them boys'd look at it. Then she goes and lays right down smack in front of them. They'd of had to trip on her if they wasn't starin at her. And that's with me, her little sister, being with her, for Pete's sake. Hate to know what she does when little sister ain't there. Probably really flashes her stuff, I bet."

It was just teasing. Gretchen figured that by the time you get to be as old as her sister, you ought to be able to take a little joking around. But no, not Miss Hubcap Knees, not her. She had to go get carried away again over the stinking measliest little thing.

A little bit of milk dripped from big Sis's rubbery lips, but she didn't spit. She kept chewing, but something was waking up in her eyes, that was for sure. Her eyes were as big as her kneecaps.

For Pete's sake, Gretchen thought, I'm just playing around. If you can't do a little kidding around at the dinner table about your big sister, what's the world coming to anyways?

So far, their mother was handling the kidding just fine. It almost seemed to calm her down, like maybe if there was enough stirring someplace else, she didn't have to do all the stirring herself. Their father was another matter. His serious face got more serious and more serious until all the wrinkles pulled tight and pointed straight toward his upper lip. He didn't like what he heard in this sandpit talk.

"You do need a different bathing suit," he said calmly to Jo-Anne. "That thing you've got isn't decent."

So maybe Gretchen had exaggerated a little bit— what's wrong with that? Somebody had to get some talking going around this table. It was kind of nice, though, seeing that Daddy didn't think it was funny. It was kind of nice seeing Daddy's pet get it in the neck for a change. Take that, Daddy's pet, Gretchen thought.

Jo-Anne did take it. She didn't have much choice with her mouth full. But even when she finished swallowing and her mouth was empty, she didn't say a word. She was wide awake now, though. No doubt about that. She was heating up like a rotten egg that's about to explode. She was probably getting so mad that she didn't dare to blurt out what she was thinking and get their father even more riled up. If there was anything that got Jo-Anne's goat, it was when Gretchen got their father riled up. Little beads of sweat came out on his forehead when he was really bothered. And what Gretchen said about the boys at the sandpit was enough to make their father's forehead pop with a field of little sweat beads.

"Mom says we can't afford a new swimsuit," said Jo-Anne.

Aha. So that's why big Sis hadn't said anything yet. She was sitting there thinking, and this is what she had come up with. She was going to pull a fast one. She thought she had figured out a way to get a new bathing suit out of this table talk.

"She just wants to get one of them where you can see your belly button," said Gretchen.

Their mother raised her long, warning finger. "Stop it. Now."

Jo-Anne was bubbling with something, and it wasn't joy. She stood up and popped her cork. "She's always doing this!" she shouted. Her lips stuck out stiff as a fish's. "Why do you let her get away with this! You!" she went on, aiming her eyes at Gretchen. "Little Miss Big Mouth!"

Maybe this was part of what it meant to be youngest—you don't always remember what it is you've learned along life's short path, but one day you look at somebody like your older sister and for some reason new words come into your head, words you must have had stored up there for a while but have never used before.

"Hedgehog!" said Gretchen. "You're just a big-nosed hedgehog all bristled up!"

"I don't think we need this kind of talk at the table," said their father in a voice that was still steady but that you could tell was coming from someplace in his neck that was stretched tight as a slingshot pulled all the way back with a piece of sharp glass in it.

"Or anywhere else, for goodness' sake," their mother said quickly.

Gretchen stuffed some bread in her mouth.

"I'm not eating at the same table with that brat!" Jo-Anne shouted, and started to march out of the room.

"You stay for closing devotions," said her mother. "What kind of godless place is this turning into anyhow!"

"Sit down and we'll pray," said their father.

This is another way that prayer can work, Gretchen remembered. It's not just a way of trying to get something that you want or to get rid of something you don't want. It's really a good way to let bad feelings settle down. This wasn't the first time that closing devotions after a family fight was like.an ice cube in hot water.

When her father finished with his usual "thank yous" to the Lord for giving them this day and this food and their health and for the honor of gathering before Him as a family, he wiped his forehead and turned to Jo-Anne. "I'd like to talk to you first," he said. "And then you, young lady," he added, looking at Gretchen.

Gretchen heard them talking on the porch. It was mostly her father, in his low calm-sounding voice. What a fuss over nothing. And even if her sister was getting a scolding, it wasn't Gretchen's fault. Their father had said himself that Jo-Anne's bathing suit wasn't decent. Even if Gretchen had been teasing, it wasn't her fault that their father saw what he saw.

In a few minutes Jo-Anne walked through the kitchen and went upstairs. Now it was Gretchen's turn. "I want you to listen to me very carefully," he said to her. "I'm only going to tell you this once. That old couple are God's children too, and it is not right for us to hate them. But the boy's father told me that they are not right with the Lord. They do not worship. They do not honor the Sabbath. You may go there and feed their lamb. That is right in God's eyes. But do not be tempted by their strange ways. You have been taught in the ways of truth. Do not depart from them, my child. Do you understand what I am saying?"

"Yes, Father," said Gretchen.

"Do you know what is right?"

"Yes, Father," said Gretchen.

With that, her father put on his cap and headed off for the fields. Jo-Anne must have listened for the tractor to get past the second gate. That's when she came downstairs, dressed.

"I'm never going out in public with that little runt-faced brat again," she said. "I won't be seen with her. I refuse. If somebody else sees her with me, I'll swear I've never seen her before in my life. You little snot-nose creep," she said.

"Stop it!" their mother shouted. "No more fighting in this house ever again! We'll get you a new bathing suit as soon as we can afford it."

"What?" said Gretchen.

"You brat!" shouted Jo-Anne. She was moving straight toward Gretchen. Gretchen started moving slowly around the table, pulling chairs behind her as she did. Then she laid another one on her sister: "Maybe you just smelled bad and all them boys was sniffin around you to find out where the stink was comin from."

That almost blew the freckles right off Jo-Anne's face.

The chase around the table became a whirlwind of fast-legged girls.

"Not this again!" shouted their mother, and she was a windmill of flailing arms, trying to catch each of the girls as they whizzed by. "I won't have it! Oh Lord, you two will be the death of me yet."

The two girls stopped across the table from each other, each holding the back of a chair and giving no indication which way they would bolt next. "At least when you're my age you won't have to worry about boys looking at you," said Jo-Anne. "Four Eyes."

"Enough," pleaded their mother. She grabbed Jo-Anne's shoulders. "You act your age," she said.

Jo-Anne didn't try to pull away, but she said to Gretchen, "Horse Teeth."

Four Eyes would have been bad enough, but Horse Teeth? That was too much. Jo-Anne landed that one on Gretchen and then thought she could turn and go on her way. Her mother wasn't even going to scold Jo-Anne for saying something like that to her very own little sister. Her mother was going to let it go, just let it go right like that! Her mother walked back to the kitchen sink as if Jo-Anne hadn't even said anything terrible.

"Not so fast, Creepyolee," said Gretchen as her sister cruised toward the stair door. Gretchen grabbed a spoon off the table and heaved it at her. It missed and hit the stair door.

Jo-Anne laughed, but it wasn't just an ordinary teasing laugh. It was a horse laugh. Jo-Anne neighed at her is what she did.

Gretchen didn't know what she picked up off the table next, but whatever it was, she threw it as hard as she could at her horse-face neighing sister's head.

The scream that Gretchen had heard come out of her sister's mouth in North Dakota when she stepped on a broken beer bottle in the town park at the Sunday-school picnic the summer before was nothing compared to the screech she yelped out this time. It was a blood-curdler. It was one for the record books, least ways in the kitchen. It was great.

But that little nip of a second when Gretchen felt good about her sister's howl ended when she saw the blood and her sister's hand going up to cover her eye. On the floor she saw the weapon that had done the damage. It was a fork. She had taken her sister's eye out with a fork.

Gretchen whimpered an "I didn't mean it" through the howling, but what did it matter what she meant or didn't mean? This was the end of the world for her. In the short run or in the long run, she had had it. In the short run, it would mean the worst whipping ever felt by any girl in the world, followed by a half-blind sister for the rest of her life. That was the short run. In the long run, it would mean hell for sure.

"Get your hand down! Get your hand down! I can't see how bad it is!" her mother was yelling.

When her sister pulled her hand away, the whole eye was going to fall out, Gretchen was sure of it. It would fall out, a big, punctured, bloody glob on the floor. Then the hospital and a glass eye. Then the whipping. Probably a hundred whippings. Hell couldn't come soon enough.

"Oh, it's not so bad," her mother was saying.

Was she really saying that?

Her sister was cry-screaming in a big teary "Oh! Oh! Oh!"

"I knew something like this was going to happen sooner or later," her mother said. "Now let me clean that off. Stop crying. It's just four little punctures."

"Four little punctures!" howled Jo-Anne.

Gretchen watched her mother dab the four little oozing spots of blood from her sister's cheekbone. Gretchen had missed going to hell by about a half inch.

"I'm sorry," said Gretchen.

"Just go," said her mother. "Just go. Go ride your bike. Just go."

Gretchen went upstairs for her shoes. Then she put on her glasses and looked at herself in the mirror. She was ugly. She guessed she deserved to look ugly, so she kept her glasses on.

"One Band-Aid should cover it," her mother was saying as Gretchen came back down the stairs. She walked slowly across the kitchen and closed the porch door quietly as she left. She really was sorry about this, even if her sister did deserve it.

Gretchen pedaled down the driveway, then veered off toward the grove. She'd spend a little time in her treehouse. As she made her way into the cool shade of the grove, she heard her sister playing the piano. She wasn't just playing the piano, she was pounding it. "A Mighty Fortress Is Our God" came booming through the summer air. Jo-Anne was getting lots of notes wrong, but she wasn't stopping.

Gretchen sat down in her treehouse, looking out toward Henry's place. She saw him pedaling very slowly down the road toward the intersection.

Even from this distance, Gretchen could see Henry's sadness in the slow way he pedaled. She could see it and feel it because she knew it must be the same kind of sadness she was feeling. She climbed down the tree and pedaled off to meet him. She would pedal slowly too, so that he'd know how she was feeling. They wouldn't have to say anything. And if she said anything at all, she'd make sure it wasn't anything that would start an argument. Good friends are too hard to come by, she thought. I'll never argue with him again my whole life. Maybe we can just play follow-the-leader with our bikes the way we did the first time we met at the intersection.

———

SIXTEEN

"Buster! Buster! Buster!"

HENRY AND GRETCHEN THOUGHT the day had reached rock bottom, but it hadn't. They met at the intersection, their faces drooping from their sadness, their clothing drooping from the heat.

"Your folks know too, right?" said Henry.

"That ain't the worst part of the day," she said. "I just about took my sister's eye out throwin a fork at her. I didn't get a whuppin yet, but I bet I get one later."

"I got my butt kicked already for bein in my mom and dad's bedroom," he said. "I'm just takin a nap in there and Dad comes in and blows his lid."

"Get your butt kicked just for bein in somebody's bedroom?" said Gretchen. "That's about as bad as my house. Good grief."

"Same old story," said Henry.

They rode around the intersection a couple more times, and then without any warning Gretchen started pedaling toward the old couple's house. She stood, pumping hard for a minute, then settled back on her seat and swung her arms out straight, cruising along with no hands. Henry pumped hard in the smooth tire track next to her, then sat back on his seat and threw his arms out too. They touched hands, then locked fingers. At first they wobbled and were tempted to grab their handlebars, but found that they didn't have to if they leaned a little bit away from each other.

"It's easier goin with no hands if you're holdin on to somebody!" Gretchen yelled.

The way they were doing it, it was easier. They continued on, neither of them with their hands on the handlebars, one arm out free in the warm summer air, the other stretched out and holding on to the other's hand.

When they got to the base of the big hill where the old couple lived, they let go and took their handlebars again so that they could pedal hard for the final uphill push.

"We're sweating like a couple of pigs," said Gretchen once they were there.

"Pigs don't sweat," he said back.

"You know what I mean."

"Yeah," he said. "I know what you mean."

Sixer was growing, and the wool on her back was getting thicker. The extra legs weren't growing at the same rate, but seeing them hanging there was starting to seem normal to Henry and Gretchen. They were like a cowbell that an old cow always has around her neck. Pretty soon you can't imagine what she would be like without it. And like a cowbell, Sixer's extras had their own peculiar sound, a muffled tapping-against-each-other sound as she trotted toward them.

"Think we're feedin her too much?" said Henry.

"Not hardly," said Gretchen. "They're supposed to put on fat and wool like this. Come 'ere, Sixie Sixie."

Sixer was her usual friendly self as Henry and Gretchen got down to pet her. The lamb nuzzled them, nuzzled and sniffed, then licked at Henry's sweaty face. In a few minutes, the old man came by and stood watching them.

"What'd you bring?" he said, looking around in the straw.

They'd forgotten. They'd forgotten to bring anything new. No food for the old couple, no feed for Sixer. Of course, the old couple had to be counting on it. Why shouldn't they? Henry and Gretchen had been making such a regular point of showing off what they brought each time.

They looked at each other, and then at the old man.

"We forgot," said Gretchen. "We just plain forgot. We're feelin bad and we forgot."

"Not next time," said Henry. He was already thinking of the canned meat that looked like it was lost in the back of the pantry shelves.

"Feeling bad," said the old man. "Feeling bad is bad for you, a real bad thing to do, yah. So don't do that. We got plenty of food for a while. It's the geese mostly that we're runnin short on. Yah."

"We'll fix you up good next time," said Gretchen. "Real good."

"Come on! Yoo-hoo!" It was the old woman. She was inviting them in. Maybe she was hoping for some extra supplies too.

Henry and Gretchen followed the old man toward the house. There wasn't the least thing scary about him today. His limp even looked like it was getting worse. First getting in trouble at home, and now disappointing the old couple. The day couldn't go downhill much farther. At least Sixer had been her usual happy self.

The table wasn't set when Henry and Gretchen went into the house, but the kitchen counter was covered with fixings.

"This way, this way," said the old woman. She was talking to Gretchen. "We're going to do some cooking together today. What you say, Miss Sunbeam? I'm making Rice Krispies Treats. When I saw you coming, I thought today is the day Miss Sunbeam makes Rice Krispies Treats. Now, weren't you going to bring some more butter?"

"Oh no!" said Gretchen. "We forgot! But I can get some real fast. Come on, Henry, let's go!"

Henry followed her out and they took off spitting dust with their bicycles. "Why you need me to get butter?" he said.

"I figured maybe when we got to the intersection you could go to your house and I could go to mine. That way if one of us can't sneak some butter out of the house, maybe the other one can."

"Good idea," said Henry. "Granny's always puttin a wad of butter in everything she makes."

As they came down the last stretch to the intersection, they heard the rumbling roar of a big vehicle coming. They slowed down and moved off to the side of the road. Everything happened so fast after that. They saw the cloud of dust billowing up behind the loud roar of the gravel truck. They stood next to their bikes and watched it blustering past, but it was only a second before the truck skidded for a few feet, its tandem rear wheels dragging on the packed gravel. Then the *wh-whumping* of the large animal churning beneath it. With that, the brake lights of the truck went off and the driver sped on. Whatever it was the truck had hit looked as if it was floating up off the ground as the dust cleared. But it wasn't floating. It was stretched out flat across the middle of the road.

"What's that?" said Gretchen.

He knew what it was. It was Buster. But it couldn't be Buster. Buster never went roaming like a stray dog. Buster never did anything he wasn't supposed to do.

"Looks just like Buster," he said, "but Buster don't go past the corner."

"Your big dog Buster?" said Gretchen.

"That's Buster," he said. "That's Buster. He must have gone past the intersection." Henry yelled. As loud as he could he yelled, "Buster! Buster! Buster!"

The dog didn't move.

They scrambled out of the ditch. They ran. They ran hard.

For this. For a large yellow dog with a pool of blood under his head. For what had been Buster. For a large animal with his eyes popped out. For the dizzy minute of horror. For the smell of dust. For the smell of blood on the gravel. For the sound of the gravel truck speeding on in the distance.

Gretchen let out a quick groaning sob. Then stopped. Henry was silent.

"They're gonna blame me," he said. "Look. Buster must've gone down the ditch to see what we was hidin in the grove for the old couple. He must've smelled something we put there. He was checkin it out."

"They can't blame you," said Gretchen. She looked at him now.

Henry kept looking at the dog. He bent over and lifted Buster's front paw, held it, and dropped it.

"Guess we been praying for the wrong thing," he said.

He stood there. He just stood there. She watched him.

"My mom was good with animals," said Henry. "I remember when Buster was a little pup, she taught him to stay away from the road."

Gretchen moved close to him. "We had twelve kittens one time in North Dakota," she said. "They all died of the distemper."

"We used to have another dog, a little rat terrier named Skippy," said Henry. "He was Buster's little friend. Last year he run away and never come back."

"We still got Sixer," said Gretchen.

Henry kept staring at Buster. "I wish I was a town

kid," he said. "Wouldn't always have to be lookin at another dead animal. Every time you turn around, there's another dead one. I hate it. I ain't never gonna have another pet. Never."

"I wish I could bring him back for you," said Gretchen.

"Ain't nothin we can do," said Henry. "Dead is dead. We gotta get him off the road or there's gonna be a accident." He bent down to take both front paws. "I'm gonna pull him off the road."

Gretchen watched him pull. She bent down and took the hind legs. They dragged the dead dog off the road. They stood alongside the road and looked at what had been Buster. Gretchen looked at Henry, and when he turned away to head back toward their bicycles, she followed him, a half step behind.

At first the tears just rolled down Henry's face as they walked, then came a soft whining cry from his closed mouth. He cried through his nose. She reached for his hand, but it didn't turn toward hers. She took his wrist. She walked beside him holding his wrist as he kept his lips pinched tight and howled through his nose. They sat down in the grass with their feet in the ditch. She put her arm around his shoulder and pulled him toward her. He put the top of his head against her cheek, leaned toward her, and wept.

SEVENTEEN

Saving the Day

IF IT HADN'T BEEN for the old couple, the day might have turned out even worse, if that could be possible. When a half hour had gone by and Henry and Gretchen still hadn't come back with butter to make the Rice Krispies Treats, the old man came down a path that he must have known about in the grove and stepped out of the thick underbrush into the ditch right where Henry and Gretchen were sitting. When he found out what had happened, he worked his way down through the ditch on his crippled leg, walked over to Buster, and studied the dog for a few minutes. Then he walked back, patted each of them on the head, and said, "Don't have to talk about it right now, just come."

He had picked up Henry's and Gretchen's bikes and started steering them, one in each hand, up the road and toward the old couple's driveway. Seeing this, Henry and Gretchen had gotten up and caught up with him. They got on their bikes and pedaled slowly down the worn tire paths as the old man shuffled along on the shoulder. The old woman was waiting outside the house. She stood studying them as if she knew something terrible had happened.

She had lemonade on the table by the time the three sad-looking people came into the house. She put the Rice Krispies Treat makings back in the cupboard and brought out some bread. She handed the old man the teeth, then walked over to Gretchen. She put her old hands on the girl's forehead and gently rubbed back over her hair, pulling the ponytail through her hands with each stroke.

"That big dog, the boy's Buster," said the old man. "Monsters out there, my idea of it. Gravel truck."

The old woman walked over to Henry. "It hurts," she said. "I know it hurts. Don't listen to people who say it doesn't. It hurts and it will get better. But it hurts."

What followed was twenty minutes of silence. Looking down. Looking out the window.

"Now we can eat," said the old woman. She used the peanut butter she had out for Rice Krispies Treats and placed sandwiches in front of everyone. She didn't say anything. She just fed them.

Just exactly what it was the old couple had done to make things easier was never quite clear to Henry and Gretchen, but when they rode home, it was as if the very worst part was over. And there was no finger-pointing at home. No blame for what happened to

Buster. When Gretchen explained that Henry's big dog had been killed by a gravel truck, Jo-Anne actually fixed supper and then cleaned up the supper dishes. At Henry's house, Jake and Josh passed Henry food at the table first, without even making sure they got the biggest piece of everything.

Granny was taking Buster's death the hardest, crying when she talked about how that dog hadn't even had the chance to know what it feels like to get old. But her crying stopped when Henry started looking like he might be shedding some tears himself. She fed him good.

Then, after supper, Granny showed that feeding Henry was not the only way she knew how to be nice. "Come down to the basement with me," she said to him.

This was the first time Granny had ever invited Henry down there. He hoped she wasn't going to choose this terrible time to warn him about sneaking down there and taking ice cream and cookies from her refrigerator. She wasn't.

"Over here," she said, and led Henry to the little chest of drawers next to her sewing machine. She sat down on her sewing chair with a heave, then leaned down over her big stomach and pulled open a drawer. There inside was a stack of big brown photograph albums, almost as many as he had found in his dad's room.

"This one," she said, and opened an album. Inside were pictures of Buster. Buster as a pup. Buster with a ribbon around his neck. And there was one of Buster with the little rat terrier, Skippy, who had disappeared over a year ago. The next picture was of Henry playing with Buster on the lawn. That had to be last year, after Skippy disappeared.

"And I have one very special one," said Granny. She opened another photo album, and on the front page was a picture of Buster, Henry, and his mother together, sitting on the front porch. Buster looked like a puppy in this picture. So did Henry. Granny's hands shook a little, and she slowly closed the album.

Seeing Granny with all these pictures reminded Henry that for all her flobby lying around, Granny was the picture-taker of the family. He had hardly ever noticed, and it wasn't something he'd ever really thought about until just now. Of course, Granny always brought out her Brownie camera when you least expected it.

For a half hour Henry sat with Granny as she talked about Buster, and let him talk about Buster, pulling out even more pictures of the dog and telling a little story about each one. So many of these pictures were ones that Granny must have taken before his mother died. She must have been spending an awful lot of time here long before his mother died. Maybe everybody knew it was coming. Maybe Granny had been getting ready for his mother's death long before it happened.

The telephone was busy the next day, and it was only after Buster was dead that Henry and Gretchen learned that their parents had been talking on the telephone almost every time they got together. The telephone. Of course. But now their parents were saying that they thought it would be just fine if Henry and Gretchen used the telephone too. They didn't have to go watching for each other when they wanted to get together. They could just make a telephone call.

At least nobody was asking questions about the old couple. Nobody was saying that it might not be a good idea to be going over there so much and risk catching the craziness that the grown-ups were so afraid the old couple might spread around the neighborhood.

Henry's and Gretchen's folks even went one step further. They had decided that it would be all right for each of them to go over to the other one's house for snacks now and then. Sure, they could still go and feed their pet lamb at the old couple's house, but why not come on over for some lemonade or Popsicles now and then?

For Henry and Gretchen this was a double treat. They weren't going to stop going over to the old couple's house for the old woman's goodies, but what was wrong with having two snacks in an afternoon? Nobody would have to know.

The next day Gretchen visited at Henry's house for the first time, and she hadn't been there very long when something strange happened. Stranger than anything that had ever happened at the old couple's house.

They were sitting at the kitchen table drinking lemonade and eating cookies when Henry's father came in the house with the older brothers right behind him.

"We've got a problem," said Henry's father, "and

you're the only one who can help. We've got to move fast."

He was looking at Henry. Then he looked at Gretchen. "You don't have to watch this if you don't want to," he said. "You can go home if you want to."

"Do I gotta?" she said. "What's going on anyways?"

A sow was littering in the hog house but something had gone wrong. Real wrong. Henry's father said they needed his small hands to help with the problem. He had skinnier arms than the rest of them and could get inside to stop the bleeding. It had to be done right now before the sow bled to death.

"You gotta go inside?" said the girl. "We had this cow couldn't have her baby in North Dakota, but the feet was stickin out, so we just tied a rope on those feet, and me and my sister and Dad, we just lugged that little critter right out."

"This is different," said Henry's father. "You don't have to stay if you don't want to. It isn't pretty. Come on, come on, come on."

He was heading out the door.

"I wanna," said the girl. "Can I?"

"She can handle weird stuff," said Henry, then checked himself quickly. He didn't want any questions like "What weird stuff, for example?"

"Whatever," said Henry's father. He was running toward the hog house. "Come on!" he yelled. "Come on!"

Henry and Gretchen ran too, getting there with Henry's brothers. The sow was a large Chester White, penned up in the farrowing pen, which wasn't much bigger than the space inside a car if you took all the seats out. Two little pigs had already been born. One was nursing and the other was dragging his stringy umbilical cord between his wobbly newborn legs and pushing himself along toward the big ripe nipples that waited two feet away. Next to the pen lay a piece of #9 wire that Henry's father had bent to have a little fingerlike hook on the end. The sow had been having trouble delivering this second pig, and because the birth canal on this sow was so small that Henry's father and older brothers could not work their arms inside to grab the head of the wedged pig, Henry's father had used this wire contraption to hook the stuck pig under his chin and pull him out. It was always a last resort. "Going fishing for them" is what his father called it.

The pig had been born all right and you could hardly notice the little spot of blood where the wire hook had gone through the bottom of his chin, but the hook had done some damage to the inside of the sow. A steady trickle of blood flowed from the rear of the sow into the straw.

"It's a blood vessel or something," said Henry's father, already down on his knees behind the sow. "Every time she pushes, trying to have another pig, that blood comes pouring out. Go in there. See if a pig is stuck in there. Maybe we clear the tube and the bleeding stops. Go in there. Now."

It wasn't as if there was any time to think about this, which was probably a good thing. It wasn't something you wanted to think about. It would be a good idea if the talking stopped too.

Henry felt his heart thunking. He sat on his knees looking at the sow. You could see the contractions rippling across her long rib cage. Every time she pushed, the blood came out faster.

"Well, you going to do it or aren't you?" said his father.

Henry looked up at Jake. Big tough-guy big brother stood there like a scared wimp. "I cain't get in there. I tried," Jake said.

"Me neither," Josh said, and swallowed, as if for the first time he was choking on all his smart-alecky words.

This was how it was going to be. As the youngest kid, Henry had been here before. That good old double-bind. One minute everybody's telling you what you can't do because you're too little. They just want you to get out of the way, as if they wished you didn't exist at all. Then all of a sudden they hook you with one of these. Was this going to be punishment for being little, or a chance to show you had grown up? This was worse than the hump. This was worse than being blamed for snitching fudge. This was the long and short of it. This is what being youngest was all about.

"All right," said Henry. His father parted the sow's opening and Henry's hand disappeared inside.

He was only wrist-deep when he felt the source of the blood, like the end of a soft straw or a strand of cooked spaghetti. He put his finger on the source and little spurts of blood licked the tip of his finger.

"Found it," he said. "Right here. I can feel it spittin blood."

He took the end of the vessel between his fingers and

pinched. "Got it," he said. The sow heaved again in the middle of a contraction. No new blood appeared.

"I can feel another pig comin," said Henry. "I can feel its nose on my knuckles. It's comin! It's comin! It's slidin right over my hand!"

"Hang on to that vessel, just hang on," said his father.

"Here it comes! Here it comes!" shouted Henry. "It tickles."

With that, a tiny white pig slid along Henry's forearm and into the straw.

Gretchen was down on her knees beside Henry. "Oh, look at it," she said. "Look at it, the sweet little thing."

The sweet little thing was covered with the slimy film of its birth sac, its snout breaking through and its tiny, moist eyes opening, blinking, and feeding into its mind its first light and its first view of the world, which was Gretchen's bespectacled face leaning over it.

"Hang on to that vessel," said his father.

"Here comes another one!" said Henry. "Oh man, does this feel weird! It's like this fat snake slidin over my arm. Oh man, here it is!"

"Those little duffers are just a-pourin out, ain't they?" said Gretchen, who was hovering right there.

"That's four, and here comes five," said Henry.

For the next half hour Henry hung on while the sow finished having her litter of pigs. Nine tiny Chester White pigs clamored and nudged for the sow's pap. Finally the contractions stopped and a long puddle of afterbirth streamed over Henry's arm and into the straw behind the sow. Henry and Gretchen looked away as Henry's father quickly forked it up and threw it on the manure pile. Henry stayed where he was. So far so good, but now what?

"I'm gettin tired," said Henry. "My arm's like to fall off. I can't hold much longer." He looked at Gretchen, who had moved in close again now that the afterbirth was gone. He knew he had a replacement.

"I'll do it," she said. "I can do it."

"You better not," said Henry's father.

"You can't go letting her stick her hand in there," said Jake, who was suddenly getting brave again now that the tough work was done.

But Henry pulled his hand out and held the sow open before anybody could argue any longer.

"Got it," said Gretchen. "I got it. You can feel right where the blood is squirtin out."

"We'll just take turns," said Henry. He sat down on his knees next to the girl and wiped his arm with fresh straw.

The amount of blood that escaped in the short time that it took for Henry and Gretchen to switch off told Henry's father that only part of the problem had been solved. The sow could stay alive for a while, but when they stopped doing what they were doing, the sow would steadily bleed to death. He told them to hold on as long as they could while he called the veterinarian, who'd come over and tie off the blood vessel. In the meantime, Jake and Josh could go to the house and get some lemonade and sandwiches to bring back.

Alone in the hog house together, Henry and Gretchen listened to the steady happy grunting sounds of the sow as she nursed. They listened to the little squeals and slurping of the contented nursing piglets. Gretchen hung on. When she looked up at Henry, she caught his smile and she smiled too. They were alone and they were saving the day. "Ain't this great?" she said.

"Yeah," he said. "Let's not let 'em know how much fun we're havin."

EIGHTEEN

"Those Old People Are Crazy!"

THE NEXT DAY was a scorcher like none other that summer. By one o'clock in the afternoon Henry was already drenched with sweat. He put his nose toward his arm. Had the bleeding sow left him with a bad smell? That wasn't it exactly. He sniffed toward his armpit. There it was. He had never smelled a bad smell in his own armpits before. And now this heat—it was making everything worse. Your sharp sunshiny heat was one thing, but this was the muggy kind that hangs on, so thick you could cut it with a knife. Heavy heat that pushes you from all sides and won't let you move. Won't even let you break out in a good sweat, just makes everything feel sticky. Worst day of the summer, hands down.

He went back to his armpits, sniffing. He picked up

something here and there that reminded him of his older brothers on a hot day. He couldn't meet Gretchen smelling like his brothers! But the thought of a bath made the heavy wet heat feel even heavier and wetter. On days like this his brothers didn't bathe either, they used deodorant.

It was worth a try. Henry knew that Jake had cans and cans of deodorant in his room. Spray cans and roll-on cans. Yellow cans, blue cans, green cans. Let's see here. He picked up a tall green can with a spray nozzle. Sure Fire/Pine Scent. He tried it on his hands and sniffed his palms. It didn't just smell good, it made his palms cool. He lifted his shirt and sprayed everything from his waist to his elbows. He could feel the deodorant suck up the sweat. He sprayed a little on the back of his neck. He was ready. His whole body was a blooming cool pine scent against the heat and stink of the day.

Gretchen was having the same kind of trouble with the hot, muggy day. She didn't sweat much, but she was still worrying about it. The only place she ever had a problem was under her ponytail at the back of her neck, so on days like this she'd just wear it even higher than usual. Sweating is one thing, but smelling bad is another. Her sister had stinky feet, one of those yucky things about her that she tried to hide from boys by wearing clothes that drew their attention somewhere else.

Gretchen sniffed her tennis shoes. They smelled all right. But her sister could never smell her own stinky feet and couldn't tell that her shoes smelled bad too, so

Gretchen worried, Maybe my shoes stink and I don't even know it. She wasn't going to be like the old lady in church with bad breath who leaned toward you even if you leaned away from her. She got some of her sister's after-bath powder and sprinkled it in her shoes. She put on clean white socks, slipped on her tennis shoes, and stood in front of her bedroom mirror. Sweat drops bubbled up on her nose. She'd carry some toilet paper to dab away little problems like this, but why not use just a little bit of perfume to cloud up the smelly issue in case there was one?

She had her own perfume that she'd gotten from a girlfriend in North Dakota. It was too strong to wear in winter without everybody turning their noses toward her, but this was probably the one day she could use it. Nothing would smell too strong in this heat. She dug out the tiny little bottle of Little Miss Majesty. She dabbed some under her chin. On the inside of her elbows. Then she lifted her shirt and splashed some over her belly.

Her final preparation was getting together a bag full of food. More flour and sugar, a bag of pink pepper-mints, and a half bag of peas. As she left her place with her supplies strapped around her waist, she felt how heavy the pedals of her bike were. It was the heat. The air was so heavy that even on level ground it felt like pumping uphill. The telephone wires drooped low between the poles. She thought of the air as a big heavy sky weight pushing down on everything. Nothing looked bright and light the way it could on a sunny winter day. Even the corn lost its color in this steamer of a day. It looked more gray than green. The only thing that came alive was the smell of the perfume and the sharp leg-rubbing songs of the cicadas in the trees. She could almost smell the sharp cicada songs, she could almost hear the sharp smell of her perfume.

Henry had loaded himself up with feed for Sixer and the geese, plenty of oats and cracked corn stuffed in a feed sack that Granny had turned into a pillowcase. He had just turned it back into what it was supposed to be in the first place. As he set off, he wasn't sure if it was the deodorant on his skin or the smell of it all around him that made the air feel a little cooler. Little whiffs of hot air bounced off the gravel on the driveway and hit him on his cooler face. Up on the electric line, a poor little sparrow that hadn't found any cool and fragrant relief sat there on its perch, wide-beaked and panting. Itchy sweat formed on Henry's lip, but he still felt sweet and dry everywhere else. He pedaled slowly to the intersection and saw that Gretchen was on her way.

He decided it was not fair to make her look at dead Buster by herself. He pedaled faster so that he got to the intersection and then halfway to the old couple's house before she got there. When he got to the spot where Buster had been killed, he saw what had happened. Somebody had buried Buster.

"Somebody buried Buster," he said as she got there.

"It was your granny," she said. "Should've seen her. I saw your car parked out there yesterday, so I starts headin out on my bike. Then I seen it was your granny with a spade. Thought it was like to kill her, the way she was pumpin away with that spade, her big old blubbery belly just a-bouncin every time she hit her foot down. Then she seen me and I turned back."

"She is a fat one, ain't she?"

"She's a fat one," said Gretchen. "She was tryin to be nice, though, don't you think?"

"Guess so," said Henry. "Guess Granny was tryin to be nice for a change."

Henry looked at Gretchen and felt the tears coming. Her eyes got glassy too, but she didn't cry. They didn't move toward each other to hold each other. That was not why they came to meet. Buster was dead and buried now. That was over.

They went into the grove with their supplies. They saw that they were only a few feet farther than Granny had been when she buried Buster.

"We gotta hide these better," said Henry. "Let's put them in the grove a little farther."

"You're right," she said. "We don't want nobody findin this stuff exceptin us."

They picked up their supplies and started moving deeper into the grove. It was a thick grove, but they pushed and kicked and shoved, slowly making their way a little deeper into the tangled bushes and fallen branches.

"Next time this will be easier," said Henry as he swiped and kicked and broke off twigs. "How the heck did the old man get through here? He must know a better way."

Gretchen looked back. "We couldn't get lost in this mess, could we?" she said. "I mean, we don't got no water with us or nothin. We better break more branches and leave us a trail."

"We're breakin branches," said Henry. "Just look at that hole we're makin. You could get a cow through it."

He pushed his way through a little farther, until he came upon a small clearing, almost like a deserted campsite, and in the middle of the clearing was a dead animal. A little dog. Henry stepped closer and bent down over the dog.

"It's Skippy," said Henry. "This is the little rat terrier I told you about."

"Not another dead dog!" she screamed. "Not another one!"

They both swallowed. It was not a pretty sight.

Skippy had been so small he could stand up straight under Buster's belly without touching him. Now, here he was, right where he had probably been the whole time he was gone.

Henry and Gretchen kept looking. How did Skippy get out here, dead? This was the old people's grove.

What was left of Skippy didn't smell. Nothing had tried to eat him either. He had dried up like the leaves around and under him. Skippy looked like he was making his way into the ground, as if to dig his own grave. The leaves where he lay looked like an old couch that starts to sag from somebody sleeping on it all the time. Skippy's eye sockets had sagged in too, and his top lip had dried up, so you could see his pointy little rat terrier teeth, but his skin was still black-and-white Skippy. Henry put his finger on Skippy's stomach. That wasn't skin. It was more like cowhide.

"Lookit that," said Henry. He pointed to a small hole in the dog's rib cage. "Betcha that's what killed him."

He picked up a front paw. Skippy didn't have any joints anymore, and the whole body moved like a piece of two-by-four when he lifted.

"Bet there's another hole on the other side just like this one," he said. He flipped the tiny dog over. Leaves and dirt turned over with the stiff body.

"See?" he said.

"Somebody shot him," said Gretchen. "That's a bullet hole, ain't it? That's a bullet hole, and it went right through his poor little body and come right out the other side."

"That or a pitchfork," said Henry.

"What's that? What's that over there?" Gretchen pointed.

There were more animal remains. A wing and feathers. Goose feathers. And the head of what must have been a little red pig. This was more than a clearing where Skippy lay dead. This was an animal cemetery, and they were standing in the middle of it. The breeze through the trees got louder. Gretchen felt it like a hand pushing her toward the dead animals. She stepped back. There was more than dead animals here. This was like standing someplace where death has been sniffing around for anything it could find, gathering creatures in its sticky hands.

They both looked back at the opening they'd come through. Then they saw another opening through the bushes, and a path. This path aimed straight in the direction of the old couple's house.

Henry and Gretchen looked at each other, their eyes glowing.

"I'm scared," said Gretchen.

"Let's get out of here," said Henry.

"Your dad was right, wasn't he?" said Gretchen. "Those old people are crazy!"

Just when they had come to trust the old couple again! Just when they were thinking that everybody was wrong about them! They had been so nice lately that Henry and Gretchen had forgotten they'd ever been afraid of them. Was all that friendliness just a trap the old couple was laying for them? Now what? They'd run into dead ends like this before, and they didn't have a plan now that they'd got here. But they did have their trusty last resort. They called on it. They ran. They ran like mad.

NINETEEN

Tornado Alley

WHEN THEY GOT OUT of the grove, they sat drenched in sweat and huddled in the ditch, where gnats stuck to their moist hair and tiny gray weed seeds drifted into their noses.

"Why did we have to see something like that?" said Gretchen. "The heat's bad enough. Maybe on a nice cool day my stomach could handle that." She wiped her forehead with her hand, then wiped her hand on her knee.

Henry sat beside her breathing deep. A few feet away red ants scurried over the dark loam that was Buster's grave.

"What if the old couple really are crazy?" she said. "What if they just kill things and probably don't even know why?"

"Let's just think, let's just think," said Henry. "We've been wrong a couple times about things."

They climbed out of the ditch to the side of the road, where a faint breeze touched their faces. Henry swung his hat at a horsefly that buzzed around Gretchen's head. "Let's talk about this," he said. "Let's think real hard and talk."

In the sweltering heat, they talked. They wiped sweat from their faces and they talked. The longer they talked, the darker their thoughts got. What if getting locked in the upstairs with the geese wasn't really an accident? Maybe the old couple were practicing for the day when they wouldn't unlock the door. What if giving them Sixer was just a way of getting them in the habit of coming over there? Get their guard down and then one day, *zip*, a knife in your guts and you'd be dumped out there with Skippy. And why did everybody call them the crazy old couple? Could everybody be wrong? They didn't always seem so crazy. Most of the time they seemed like the sweetest old people you'd ever want to meet. But maybe that was part of the plan—not acting so crazy so they could catch you when you weren't expecting anything. And what about those brown-sugar sandwiches that made them feel sick? What about a lot of things?

They talked themselves into the darkest corners of fear. They couldn't tell anymore if they were sweating because it was so hot out or because they were so scared. What would it be like to be eaten by another person? Chewed on and swallowed like a pork chop? But it was this question that also let some light into the dark corner of fear: "If'n the old man had the teeth, he'd eat you first," said Gretchen, "and if'n the old lady had the teeth, I'd be a goner."

With that they started to laugh, and the bad thoughts that had been flying through their minds like big ugly vultures started soaring off and out of their minds. But when the laughing stopped, the vultures came back again.

"Maybe Sixer's a wolf in lamb's clothing," said Gretchen.

With that, the laughter came back and the vultures of fear gave up their attack. "Oh man," said Henry when they stopped laughing, "they're probably not bad. They're just old and nuttier than fruitcakes." He started laughing again. "If'n the old man had the teeth, I'd be first to go! That's a good one!"

"I ain't scared no more," said Gretchen. She stood up and looked down the road to the intersection.

"I'm not afraid to go back," said Henry.

"Me neither," said Gretchen. "Let's just go over there and ask them."

While they were biking toward the old couple's place, though, a few flickers of fear did come back.

"It don't make no sense, Skippy being dead out there," said Henry.

"Don't get me scared again," said Gretchen. "Let's just ask. We can stay on our bikes if we're not sure, so we can take off if it turns out the old man kills things for the fun of it. We'll just take off."

"And then maybe sneak over there and take Sixer and hide her someplace."

"Right," said Gretchen. "Hide her in one of those big culverts and go over there and feed her. We could easy do that."

As they biked down the driveway to the old couple's house, they saw the old man stooped over near the barn. There must have been more nails to pick up in that yard than there were strawberries to pick in the garden. He was wearing his long-sleeved shirt and even in this heat didn't show any signs of sweating.

Henry got off his bike and stood beside it, ready to jump on and take off if that's what he'd have to do. "We found Skippy in the grove," he announced straight out.

The old man set his nail bucket down. He looked at Henry. "Ach, yah," he said. He took his cigar out of his mouth, spit on the ground, and put it back in the corner of his mouth. "I always liked it when Skippy came around here," he said. "Poor little thing."

"You knew about it, then? You knew that dog was dead with a bullet hole in him?" said Gretchen. She gave him a spit-fiery look and set her foot on her bike pedal, her front wheel aimed toward the road.

The old man didn't have the teeth. He was working his cheeks. The unlit cigar between his lips waved in the air.

"No guns," he said. "Poor little thing. He went and ate this dead rat. Full of rat poison. Blood comin' out of his little mouth, you see."

The old man put his hand to his cheek.

"You sayin Skippy ate poison from a dead rat?" said Henry. "You didn't kill him because he was makin a nuisance of himself around here, diggin in the garden or somethin? We seen this hole in him. We seen it."

"Pitchfork," said the old man. "That little dog was choking on his own blood. I tried to put him out of his misery. I did the best I could. Yep. Poor little feller." He sniffed and rubbed his nose. "More'n a year now." The old man's lips pinched down hard on his cigar.

"Why didn't you tell nobody if it was a accident?" said Henry.

"Ach," said the old man. "That would just make everybody sad. No sense talking about it."

"There's other dead animals out there," said Henry.

"Yah," said the old man. "I can't go throwing those poor things out on the fields like manure when they die. Can't do that. Animals aren't manure you can just go throwing out on the field." He chewed on his cigar again. He spit in the dirt. "It ain't right," he said. "I cleared out that place for them in the grove."

"We seen it," said Gretchen. "It's scary."

"Yah," said the old man. "I was going to dig holes for them, but there's so many roots in the ground there. And my hip, you know. Too bad. And you seeing both your dogs dead in one week. Awful thing to happen to a good boy like you," he said. He was feeling so sad he couldn't look at them.

"We'll just go play with Sixer," said Gretchen. "We still got Sixer."

When they got in the barn, Gretchen said, "Wasn't that sad? I thought he was gonna cry."

"Old man ain't never hurt nothin, that's for sure,"

said Henry. Sixer came bouncing toward them. She kicked her hind legs in the air and let out a "baa" that anyone could tell was her way of saying hello. The extra legs hadn't changed any, but the rest of her was as wonderful as ever.

They checked out the extras again, rubbing the spot where they were attached to the lamb's shoulders. "They're still just hangin there," said Henry. "They're just hangin there by skin. I still think we could find somethin to fix her."

"I'm thinkin Sixer maybe ain't no fixer-upper," said Gretchen. "It ain't her fault she got borned like this, but it's what she turned into. Who'd want to be born with some freakish legs hangin under your chin anyways? Ain't her fault. It just happened, that's all."

"Like if somebody got born with big ears or somethin?" said Henry.

"That's exactly what I'm sayin," said Gretchen. "God planned it that way is what I'm sayin."

"I dunno about that," said Henry. "That's like sayin if God planned for us to ride on bikes, He'd've put wheels on our butts."

"It ain't like sayin that," said Gretchen.

"Maybe not," said Henry.

"It's like sayin the way you got borned is the way you got borned, that's all. Take it or leave it."

"But we been tryin to fix Sixer," said Henry. "Is that so bad? You make it sound like being born with freak legs is like havin crummy brothers and sisters."

"I didn't say that," said Gretchen. "They treat you that way sometimes though, don't they?"

"I know it," said Henry.

"Hey," said Gretchen. "We forgot to bring all that stuff we was gonna hide in the grove. Let's go get it and make the old man feel better."

On their bikes and pedaling slowly through the sweltering heat back to the spot where they had left their supplies, Henry told Gretchen about Skippy. "Neighbors didn't like Skippy," he said. "He was another one got borned wrong. Always diggin stuff up and gettin in trouble about it. Dig, dig, dig—that was Skippy for you."

"There was this dog in North Dakota," said Gretchen, "he was a crazy one too. He was a runner. Always chasin after this guy's pickup because he wanted to jump on the back and have a ride. Wherever this guy went, this crazy dog would chase behind. The guy would slow down a little bit so the dog would think he was catchin up. Keep his hopes up, you see. Then when the dog almost got catched up and was gonna jump on the back of the pickup, this guy just speeded up again. Just bein mean, you know. Just teasin the dog, makin him think he could get a ride on the back of that pickup if he could just run a little bit faster."

"Did he ever catch up? I mean, did he ever get a ride on that pickup?"

"Nope. His feet wore out."

"Come on," said Henry.

"They did," said Gretchen. "This guy teased that dog to run ten miles down this tar road all the way to this one town, and when they got there the dog's feet was all bloody." She held out her hand and rubbed her palm. "Wore all this pad right off. Vet had to put that dog down."

"I don't believe ya," said Henry. "You're always sayin all these crazy things happened in North Dakota."

"It's the truth," said Gretchen. "Worse things happen around here, you ask me."

"I think you make some things up. You're the talker, you know."

"Did not make that up," she said.

Just then thunder rumbled through the sky.

"See?" said Gretchen. "God's tellin you to shut up your mouth."

"Look, lightning," said Henry. "God's tellin you to quit lyin."

"I ain't lyin," she said. "Maybe in a minute you'll be all wet. That would prove somethin."

"We get a lot bigger storms in Iowa, I bet, than you ever got in North Dakota."

"We had worse drought in North Dakota, I bet," she said. "This one time in North Dakota, it got so dry that the preacher had to baptize this one little baby with spit."

"Cut it out," said Henry.

They stopped near the spot where Buster was buried and went into the grove, to where they had left the food. As they stepped back out and into the ditch, a louder rumble of thunder boomed across the cornfields.

"That's a big one," said Henry. "We could be gettin a big storm."

Spatters of lightning cut across the clouds.

"One, two, three," said Gretchen, before a drumbeat of thunder sounded over them.

"What ya countin?" he said.

"Miles," she said. "Don't ya know about thunder? After the lightning you count, and as far as you get is how many miles away the lightning is. Sounds to me you don't know nothin about weather."

The next streak of lightning sounded like a curtain blind ripping over their heads, and the crack of thunder was on its heels.

"That was close," she said.

"Look," said Henry. "What's that if you know so much?"

They both knew what it was.

"That's a twister," she said.

"Tornado," he said.

"Twister," she said. "In North Dakota we don't call them tornadoes until they touch down. They can hang in the sky like that like a bunch of string beans. Don't mean nothin if they don't touch down."

They watched the dark funnel swing from the bottom of a low cloud on the horizon. Swing slowly like a thick kite tail.

"It ain't touchin down," she said. "I seen them swing like that."

"I seen worse tornadoes than you seen, I bet," he said.

"Bet ya ain't," she said. "We lived in Tornado Alley. More tornadoes than Carter's got liver pills out there."

"What's Tornado Alley?" said Henry.

"See, you don't know nothin about tornadoes," she said. "Tornado Alley is like this big wide alley that only tornadoes can see, and when a tornado looks down from the sky and sees Tornado Alley, it just turns right down it like a big old truck and comes roarin down on your head."

"Bet you ain't never been in a tornado," said Henry.

"No, I ain't been in one, but I seen them and I seen what they done afterward. Lots of times. Bet you ain't never been in one neither."

"Been in the storm cellar," said Henry. "And I seen what they done to other people's places. This one time a tornado come about ten miles away on top of this one farm and it just stayed there like it was mad at these people. It just jumped up and down on this one place without goin anywhere else and just smashed this whole farm to itsy-bitsy pieces. Couldn't find a board on that place that was bigger than a toothpick."

"It kill everybody?"

"Weren't nobody home," said Henry. "If they'd been home, they'd've been nothin but a grease spot."

"There's this one tornado in North Dakota went rolling down Tornado Alley about three miles away from our place, and it rolled up all the wire from the fields that were in its way, just rolled it up for miles, and when it stopped you couldn't hardly see the top of this big wad of wire."

"I'll bet," said Henry.

"It's true," said Gretchen, "and in this one place the tornado took stalks of straw and stuck them right into a tree. Buried them right in the bark of the tree. Tree looked like a porcupine when that tornado got done with it."

"This one tornado about two miles away from our house," Henry said, "it lifted these people's house right off the ground and strung the telephone wire underneath it and then set that house right back down on top of it in one piece. All the furniture and everything was all right. Just that these folks couldn't use their telephone for a while."

"That's nothin," said Gretchen. "In North Dakota at this one place a tornado took the cement basement floor right out of this house. That was the big one. It sucked up about five miles of farms and carried all kinds of stuff through the sky, and about a hunnert miles down it started puking everything back down. Wagons and dogs and television sets and what have you just come pourin out of the sky."

"I heard about that one," said Henry. "I thought that was in Kansas."

"Nope, North Dakota," said Gretchen. "But the worse one is the one that clobbered this big Catholic neighborhood. We went ridin by there after church the next day and there was bedsprings all over the fields. You couldn't hardly go nowhere because you'd run into another bedspring. They got so many kids, you know."

"You're always talkin bad about Catholics," said Henry. "It ain't right to go talkin bad about other people."

"What do you know?" said Gretchen. "You ain't never even met a Catholic. That's what you said."

"That don't make no difference," said Henry. "Catholics is just people who got grandmas and grandpas that was born in a different Old Country than ours."

"If you're so right about everything, what's that?" said Gretchen, pointing out across the fields.

They saw it together. The splash of dust and mud and uprooted corn as this tornado took root. And as it did, they felt the first cold drops of rain.

"Look how fat it got on the bottom," said Gretchen.

"It's movin," said Henry.

Like two people standing on a railroad track watching an approaching locomotive, they took a second to decide whether the fact that it was getting bigger and bigger meant that it was coming straight at them.

It was too late to go home. The only chance they had was to make it back to the old couple's place. And fast.

TWENTY

"We're Goners!"

THEY BOTH TOOK the first pump on their bikes at the same time and plowed into each other, front wheels bouncing off each other and knocking them both to the ground. Henry grabbed her arm. "We gotta hide under somethin!" he yelled.

"We can make it back to the old couple's house!" she yelled back.

They were off again, this time side by side, pedaling full-speed toward the old couple's driveway. They could see the huge dark thickness of the top of the tornado as they neared the house—and then they heard the sound that the bottom of the tornado was making as it touched the grove. Their only choice was the barn. They could make it to the barn and into the straw with Sixer. If they were lucky.

Henry switched to sidesaddle on his seat for the last ten feet. Gretchen did the same. They jumped off running and let their bikes roll on. They dropped their supplies and swung open the barn door, slammed it tight behind them, and leaped over the manger where Sixer lay in the straw. The lamb seemed to know trouble was coming and huddled down in the corner. She looked up as they ran toward her and put her head down as they fell down over her, covering her body with theirs.

"Let's get over here against the wall!" yelled Henry.

Gretchen picked up Sixer and ran to where Henry had chosen a spot against the barn wall. He put his back against the wall. Gretchen lay down in front of him, her back against his stomach and her arms around Sixer. She tucked the lamb's loose and floppy extras down under the thick wool of her chest and hung on. He put his arms over Gretchen's ribs and over Sixer's stomach. They closed their eyes and stiffened into a locked unit of boy, girl, and lamb as the tornado struck.

"Somethin sure smells good," said Gretchen.

"I thought it was you," said Henry.

She started to answer him but her voice was drowned out by the tornado rampaging the grove, ripping and tearing at the trees. They heard the snapping and cracking branches and the big *WHUFF WHUFF* sounds, as if somebody were swinging a hundred-gallon empty bucket over their heads. Little tinkling sounds got mixed in with the big roaring sounds. The tornado was like a big crazy animal charging over them and smashing every little thing in its way. Then it was like their heads were in a big bag and all the air was being sucked away. They heard a tree splattering apart and a sound like a big broom sweeping gravel. They felt as if they were on a ship going down in a storm, with everything that kept them from sinking being torn away from them. A small barn window a few feet from them popped out of its frame and away from the barn, as if it had been pulled off like a button from a shirt. The barn shuddered, setting its feet one way, then the other. They heard a ripping sound over them as if the scalp of the barn were being torn off.

"We're goners!" Gretchen said in a straight, calm voice.

"I know it," he said. "Hang on."

Like a dam that was giving way, the wall next to them moved, shoved against the back of Henry, shoved all three of them a few feet across the straw. They were inside a deep gray and mushy roar, a deep-throated sound that was punctuated by sharper cracking and splintering sounds, and then the crying out of some kind of animal, a pig or goose, and everything around them shifting and moving, things rising and settling down again quickly, along with some gentle short movements, a two-by-four wavering in the air like a blade of grass in a soft breeze and then a quick ripping as if one hand of the tornado were resting while the other was flinging about madly at anything that might be in its way. The haymow floor above them creaked and bowed like a canvas tarp and then ripped loose and was gone, opening the entire barn to the dark, churning sky above them.

Henry was no longer holding Gretchen and Sixer in

his arms. His arms were clenched against his own chest. Sixer and Gretchen were gone. He shielded his face and turned to see what was above him, and saw a large pig, lower than Gretchen's treehouse, turning in the air like a twig in a whirlpool, its legs stiff as if it were waiting to settle down, and then the animal rose in a quick twisting movement as it was sucked up deep into the sky, turning over on its back as it rose, its ears and tail flapping wildly before its entire body disappeared into the churning grayness.

And then it was over. There was no longer a barn over them. The air was ripe with the smell of freshly splintered wood and smashed tomatoes. The roar of the tornado moved off into the distance like a large semi down the gravel road. Henry moved his body, looked down to see if his legs were still there. Then he looked around at the rubble on the barn floor. Gretchen and Sixer were not there. They must have been sucked up into the sky like that pig. He moved on his hands and knees looking for any sign of them—a piece of clothing, a tuft of wool, anything. He smelled something, a smell even sweeter than his own pine scent. He pawed through the rubble, following his nose toward a section of barn wall that was bigger than a door. The piece of wall moved.

"You there?" yelled Henry. "Is that you?"

"We're over here," said Gretchen. Henry lifted as Gretchen pushed, and then there they were, both of them.

"Are you all right?" she said.

"Think so," he said. "Are you all right?"

"I can move," she said. "I think my glasses are busted."

"You got Sixer?"

"Got 'er," she said.

Henry had no idea how he had stayed alive when the entire top of the barn had been torn off, but the piece of barn wall had been like a second roof over Gretchen and Sixer. They didn't have a scratch on them. Instead of being frightened from the storm, Sixer looked calm. The lamb stood on a small patch of straw in the midst of the debris. She looked around at the splintered barn siding, sniffed at the freshly splintered wood, and then lay down, as if satisfied that all was well. She put her chin on her shoulder and seemed to be as content as the little toy lambs you see in manger scenes.

"Is she hurt?" said Henry.

"Can't be. I had her held tight against my belly the whole time, right like this," said Gretchen. She rubbed the lamb's forehead. She lifted the extra legs and looked at them. "Not a scratch anywhere," she said. "No way she could get hurt without me bein hurt. And I ain't hurt. At least I don't think so."

She looked over her arms and legs. They were smeared with mud in shades of tan to black, but there was no blood.

"You're bleedin though," she said to him.

"Where?" he said. "Don't feel nothin."

But having been told he was bleeding, suddenly he could feel the burning on his cheek. He put his hand to it and felt something sharp at the site of the pain. Gretchen came closer. "You got something stuck in your face," she said. She leaned close. "It's bloody," she said, "but there's somethin stuck in there. It's a piece of straw—that's what it looks like. A piece of straw got stuck right in your cheek." She touched it with the tip of her finger. "Like a big whopper of a sliver," she said. "I think I could get it between my fingernails."

"Do it," he said. "Pull that thing out of there. I ain't gonna have no straw growin out of my face. I'll close my eyes. Just pull that thing out of there."

She put her forearm on his shoulder to steady herself. "Here goes," she said, and with that she zeroed in on the little pipe of straw and squeezed down on it like a tweezers.

When she started to pull it out, pain shot through Henry's face. "Yi!" he yelled. "Do it!" He grit his teeth and groaned. It was like having a tooth pulled out slowly.

"Okay," said Gretchen. She held out the little spike of straw. "It was in this far," she said, and held it up to him. It was three quarters of an inch long.

"You got that out of my cheek?" he said. "That could've been my eye."

"It's what I was tellin ya about tornadoes," she said.

He put the back of his hand to his cheek. The blood was a steady stream.

"That could've been my brain," said Henry.

Gretchen flipped the straw missile into the debris. "But it wasn't," she said.

Henry noticed that his hands were shaking, like leaves on a poplar. When Gretchen saw the shaking, her lip started to tremble, and then her hands were shaking too, and then her knees. The message between them got stronger until, like a tree that is shaking with no sign of the wind, they both shuddered, their bodies vibrating and their skin suddenly cold. "I'm scared," she said.

Henry put his shaking hand to his cheek to wipe away the blood. When he started to answer her, he noticed he was short of breath. He breathed deeply. "It's over," he said. "We don't have to be scared no more."

"We could've been killed," she said.

"I know it," he said.

"Did you see that sow go flyin over?"

"I saw it," he said.

"God saved us," she said.

"I know it," he said.

"I wonder what's dead out there," she said.

"The old couple and the geese," he said. "They gotta be dead. The house comes before the barn. The house had to get it first." His teeth started chattering. "I don't dare look. Maybe Sixer should've died instead. Maybe we should've hung on to the old couple and let Sixer go flyin like that sow."

The haymow and roof of the barn were gone, and the side facing the tornado had been ripped open, and through the gaping hole Henry and Gretchen saw two carloads of people coming down the driveway, which was littered with small twigs and branches. It was their families—Jake, Josh, Granny, and his father in the first car, Jo-Anne with Gretchen's mother and father in the second car. Henry and Gretchen stepped out through the opening and looked toward the old couple's house.

There it stood, a piece of the gutter ripped loose, but still in one piece. In the downstairs window they saw the heads of the old couple peering out. Right above them in the upstairs window were the long necks of the geese. The big gander stood in the middle, lifting his wings as if he thought he was still in charge. Henry and Gretchen looked at the geese, the old couple's strange faces, then down at Sixer with her extras dangling. Their bicycles lay on the ground with their stolen supplies scattered around. Sixer sniffed at the oats and started eating from the sack Henry had dropped. Granny would recognize that sack as one of her old pillowcases. Quite a few secrets were about to come out in the open.

———

TWENTY-ONE

After the Storm

THERE'S PROBABLY NO BETTER TIME for the jig to be up than after a tornado. Everything is such a big mess, how could anybody possibly point their finger at any one thing in particular?

Being the youngest, Henry and Gretchen felt there was always a tornado waiting right around the corner to tear everything up and show the whole world exactly what they were made of. They knew it was there, but usually the ones that got them were just little twisters, little whirlwinds, really. Day after day of these little whirlwinds, making them keep their guard up. Making them keep their tongues ready to talk their way out of another one. Making them keep their legs ready to run for it.

But this had been the big one. A whole summer of little piddly tempests in a teapot wrapped into one. *Ka-blooey! Ka-blam! Ka-bonk! Snap, crackle,* and *boom!* The whole farm looked like some two-year-old had emptied his toy box.

At least the grown-ups had their attention on Henry and Gretchen as they clamored out of the cars. Gretchen's father reached her first, pulling her up in his arms and smothering her face against his chest. "Oh, Lord be praised," he said.

"Honey honey honey," said Gretchen's mother. "We just knew it was hitting here. We didn't know whether to hide in the cellar, come over here, or what! Oh oh oh," she whimpered off. "Are you all right?"

"I'm all right," she said. "We just got down and hung on. Could you hear it? It was like *whuff whuff whuff clatter bang splat,* and I seen this sow go straight up in the sky just like it was climbing Jacob's ladder. Ho!"

Henry's father put his hand on Henry's head. "Did you get under something in the northwest corner of the building like I always told you?"

"You're bleeding!" said Granny.

"Just a scratch," said Henry.

But it didn't take long for the attention to spread around the farm to notice everything else there was to see.

For starters, one of the geese let out a loud honk from the upstairs of the old couple's house.

"Holy mackerel!" said Jake. "That tornado blew them geese right upstairs there!"

About then Sixer turned toward the company, *baaed*

her greeting, and proceeded to start eating oats from Granny's pillowcase.

"My goodness," said Granny. "And it sucked one of my pillowcases all the way over here."

"And filled it with oats," said Josh.

Sixer shook her head, as if maybe she had a kink in her neck from the ordeal she had gone through. Her extras swung like loose reins on a pony.

"Oh dear! What happened to that sheep?" said Gretchen's mother. "Did the tornado do that too?"

"That sheep's a friggin freak," said Jake.

"Talk about leg a lamb, there's some leg a lamb," said Josh.

"It was wild and crazy and loud!" screamed Gretchen. "We was hidin in the barn seein that sucker comin, and did that sucker suck or what! Lookit this! Lookit this!" she yelled, pointing at the shattered barn.

"That's Sixer," said Henry to his brothers, who were warming up to Sixer. Warming up to her with smirky looks of disbelief. Henry rubbed the new blood from his cheek. "She's got six legs and we're not gonna cut 'em off."

"That's the sheep you've been feeding?" said Henry's father.

Granny waddled around. She checked Henry's bleeding cheek, looked at Sixer, looked at the house with the curious geese staring back at them, and for reasons she didn't explain to anyone, she went to the car and came back with her Brownie camera and started clicking away at everyone and everything, but especially Henry and Gretchen.

Jo-Anne had been standing tall and motionless, but now she looked around, pulled on her blouse, and said to Gretchen. "You're lucky to be alive." Then she turned her attention to Jake. "Didn't I see you at the sandpit last week?" she said, and smiled.

Henry's father stood with his hands clasped and the top part of his body rocking in slow motion as he looked around at the damage. "Providential care, providential care," he said softly over and over.

Meanwhile, the old couple stayed in place like faces inside a picture frame, staring out at the spectacle of the families gathered around Henry and Gretchen. After a few minutes of clamoring and sighing and soothing, everybody looked toward their faces in the downstairs window and the heads of the geese in the upstairs.

Granny led the way toward the house, her elbows swinging wide with each step. "Come on," she said. "We have to see if they're all right. Come on."

From the looks of things, the tornado had played hopscotch, jumping and twisting around where it wanted to. The outdoor toilet was gone, and the old doghouse was tipped over. The manure spreader that had been parked in the grove had been pulled out into the middle of the yard. The hitching bar was still right side up, but the back wheels were turned upside down. The whole thing looked like it had been twisted like a dish rag. A few shingles had been ripped off the roof of the house, but except for that and the loose gutter, the house looked untouched. The old black Chevy was in one piece, not even a window broken, but it had a branch lying across its hood.

Sixer followed everybody, stopping to sniff one of the branches that were strewn around the yard.

The old man opened the front door and came outside. "Go on in, go on in. The little woman got some stuff to eat. At least that didn't blow away. Yah." He passed by the crowd of people heading toward the house and went over to his old car. He knelt down and looked under it, first from the back and then from the front.

Jake watched him, then said, "Lose something?"

"What's not under there won't hurt you," said the old man. "Yep."

He stood up, took off his engineer's cap, pulled out a fresh cigar, and followed the others toward the house.

"Just bring Sixer on in there," he said. "There's always room for one more. Yah."

Henry went in first, looking around the room. Would some of the food he and Gretchen had brought be standing out in packages that Granny or Gretchen's mother would recognize? But before he had a chance to look around for food, he saw the false teeth. They were sitting out on the kitchen table, sitting there like a grin that had fallen out of somebody's face. His first thought was to say, "Look what else the tornado did," but instead he grabbed them off the table and hid them in his hand against his leg.

"You folks, you folks, you folks," said the old woman. "I hope you didn't get any of this weather! Come on, come on, I've got fresh bread. Eat while the eating's good."

"We watched it head straight for your farm. We knew you were getting it," said Gretchen's mother. She was hardly in the house and already she was sizing things up. She set one of the kitchen chairs straight.

"Was that you I saw stacking alfalfa bales about eight bales high out there in the field last week?" Gretchen heard her sister saying to Jake. Jake nodded shyly and smiled. Then Jo-Anne said, "I couldn't believe my eyes the way you were tossing those heavy things around. Wow."

"We'll get some neighbors together to help clean up around here," said Henry's father.

"You can always worry about today tomorrow, my idea of it," said the old man.

"The Lord works in mysterious ways," said Gretchen's father. "We have no answer for acts of God."

"Hope the Lord doesn't send any more acts of God our way," said the old woman.

"We'll help you," said Henry's father. "We'll get plenty of people over here. This neighborhood has lots of Good Samaritans."

"Hope they got pitchforks," said the old woman, who then walked out of the kitchen and into the front room. She dragged in a few more chairs and told everybody to get as close to the table as they could. Henry and Gretchen found a place for Sixer on the porch. Back in the kitchen, they sat next to each other. When the sandwich fixings were on the table, Henry's brothers dug in. Gretchen looked back and forth from the old man to the old woman. She could tell that neither one of them had the teeth and was wondering how this was going to go.

A goose honked upstairs.

"I was wondering about the geese," said Gretchen's mother.

"Them's my children," said the old woman. "Do you want to go visit them?"

"They're like kids, you know," said Gretchen. "Remember that cat lady in North Dakota? These geese are a lot cleaner."

Henry had put the false teeth in his pocket. Now he pulled them out and held them against Gretchen's leg. She reached down and he handed her the teeth and looked toward the old man.

"Oh, what's that over there?" said Gretchen, looking out the window, and when everyone looked away, she slipped the old man the teeth.

After a few minutes of eating, the old man said, "By crackie, there it goes again," and when everybody looked outside this time, he handed Gretchen the teeth under the table. She passed them to Henry, who passed them under the table to the old woman, who pretended to cover her mouth for a yawn. In a few seconds she was busy eating and no one knew the better.

When Henry and Gretchen glanced up now and then at the old couple, they saw they were smiling with their eyes.

When they finished eating, the two fathers went outside to clear some of the branches off the yard. Gretchen's mother went out to the garden with Granny to see if any of the vegetables had survived the tornado. Jo-Anne followed Jake into the grove "to see how much damage had been done there."

This left Josh by himself. In a minute he came strolling up to where Henry and Gretchen were playing with Sixer. He had a sad look on his face, which Gretchen and Henry understood. The middle boy had just been left out in the cold by his older brother. You could tell by the way he was looking at Sixer that he had learned something.

"Can I pet her?" he said.

"Sure," said Gretchen. "She's real friendly."

TWENTY-TWO

"Sweet Smells Rise"

HENRY AND GRETCHEN SAT in her treehouse watching the formless clouds drifting by. This would be the last picnic before school started. The food was nothing less than Gretchen's own Rice Krispies Treats, which followed the old woman's recipe, and a stack of fudge for which Henry had greased the pan while Granny did the fixing.

They both knew that school starting was going to change things. Henry wished the one-room schoolhouse was still open, but it closed the year Jake finished the first grade. If the old schoolhouse were still open, there'd be only a dozen students for all eight grades and it would be easy for Gretchen and him to be friends the way they were now. But at the new Consolidated

School the boys would be playing with boys and the girls would be playing with girls. They'd be on the same bus, but it wouldn't be the same, at least not until next summer, when they'd be in easy biking distance again. Until then, they'd still see each other on Saturdays, at least until the weather got too cold for biking. They'd go and feed Sixer—and they wouldn't even have to steal the oats to do it. Their fathers reminded them of that. "If you'd just learn to ask," Henry's father said. "Just ask and it shall be given."

Being youngest, Henry and Gretchen knew that nothing could be that easy. They'd still have to snitch a few things as special treats for the old couple, but it was good to know that their parents were pretty much on their side. Granny and Gretchen's mother had even agreed to send some vegetables along with them when they visited the old couple's house, since their garden had been ruined by the tornado.

Henry's and Gretchen's folks never did get over the idea of geese in the upstairs where people lived. That was the strangest thing about the old couple, as far as they were concerned. "Geese in a house," said Gretchen's mother. "That's like people sleeping in a barn." Maybe so, but the old couple didn't really seem to mean anybody any harm, at least everybody was finally agreed about that. And the matter of the false teeth was never revealed. At least one thing about them could go on without everybody making fun of it.

Sixer's extras did make for a few jokes from Henry's brothers, but nobody said they couldn't keep her as a pet at the old couple's place. There was no category for freak lambs at the 4-H fair, but they were going to show Sixer next year at the SUP show at the fairgrounds. SUP stood for Strange and Unusual Pets, and the show featured mostly miniature ponies and strange birds that should have been living in South America. But Sixer would fit in with the idea of the show. She'd no doubt get a ribbon for First in Her Class—especially since she'd be in a class by herself.

"I really like it up here," said Gretchen. "You can get above the stink of the hog yards."

"I think the leaves on the trees give off a smell, don't you?" said Henry. "I think the box elder bugs probably clean up the bark too, make everything smell sweet."

"Sweet smells rise and bad smells go down," said Gretchen. "Didn't you know that?"

"What are you talking about?" said Henry. "I never heard nothin like that before." He sniffed the air. "But some good smells sure climbed this tree."

"Bad smells go down, like cold air, and good smells go up, like warm air," said Gretchen. "Everybody knows that."

"I think you're talkin through your ear again," said Henry. "A smell is a smell and it goes wherever it wants to, up or down or crossways."

"Bad smells are heavy. They go down," said Gretchen. "Why do you think you hear people say, 'What's that heavy smell?'"

"I ain't never heard nobody say that before," said Henry.

"Listen," she said. "Close your eyes, okay? I'll prove it."

"You're kiddin me, right?"

"Just close your eyes," she said.

Henry closed his eyes.

"All right, what do you smell?" said Gretchen.

"Rice Krispies Treats," he said. "I can smell the marshmallow."

"See, I told ya," she said.

Henry opened his eyes. She was holding a Rice Krispies Treat in one hand and one of her tennis shoes in the other.

"Smell of the Rice Krispies Treat went up in your nose, and the smell of my shoe went down to the ground, where you can't smell it."

"That so," said Henry. "Well, I think you maybe gotta be right. And I'll tell you somethin else."

"What's that?" said Gretchen.

"That pig we seen go up in our tornado?"

"Yeah."

"Well, I think it must've landed in the tree right over our heads, because I just caught some real bad pig smell comin down on us, cuttin right through the sweet smells. Don't you smell it?"

She giggled and gave him a punch on the arm. "Get smart with me, mister, and I'll shove you out the tree and you'll fall to the ground like a real stinker."

"Then you'd have to stay up here, because if you went down there, you might step in it."

It was good to laugh and it was good to just sit up here quietly with the breeze moving the treehouse from side to side. Gretchen put on her glasses and looked out through the opening in the branches. The green and red combines were starting to move through the oat fields, cutting the gangly yellow stalks down to a trim and bristling stubble. The cornfields looked like rows of tired soldiers with their leafy shoulders drooping and the tassels leaning over like little bent bayonets.

"Ain't much left of summer," she said.

A meadow lark sang from the grass along the fence nearby. A brown thrasher flew near them, started to land on a branch in the next tree, then, seeing them, continued on. A few sparrows chattered from the honeysuckle bushes below them.

"Watcha thinkin about?" said Henry.

Gretchen put her elbows on her crossed legs and her hands under her chin. "I was thinkin about the owl that *whooed* that one day when I found the treehouse. I ain't seen it since then. I wonder what happened to it."

"Probably around somewhere watchin," said Henry.

"That would be all right," said Gretchen. "I don't care if somethin's watchin me as long as it ain't comin down on my head."

"Like our folks, for instance," said Henry.

"Yeah," said Gretchen. "Mine have been behavin pretty good lately."

"Mine too," said Henry. "Let's eat."

She laid out two Rice Krispies Treats on a handkerchief.

"I ain't gonna ask where you got that handkerchief," said Henry.

"Good," said Gretchen.

Henry laid out his stack of fudge. There were three pieces. "I got one extra," he said.

"I'll bet," said Gretchen. "Bet you started out with four."

"Ain't tellin," he said. He held out a piece of fudge. She looked at him, sniffed it, smiled, and took a bite. She chewed a few times, then motioned for him to take a Rice Krispies Treat.

"Whatcha waitin for?" she said.

"The teeth," he said.

They giggled, and the leaves on the tree giggled with them.